# DAVIDITY

By

John Gibson

Words Matter Publishing
P.O. Box 1190
Decatur, IL 62525
www.wordsmatterpublishing.com



ISBN 13: 978-1-953912-80-0

Library of Congress Catalog Card Number: 2022939239

# Dedication

To the junior enlisted men and
women of the U.S. military.

# ACKNOWLEDGEMENTS

Thanks to Melissa Gibson (my wife) and to
Mrs. Rhonda Dickinson for helping me edit and
proofread my manuscript prior to publication.

# Table of Contents

"This fictional story - while inspired by actual events and characters - is NOT based on a true story. Opinions and beliefs expressed herein are strictly those of the author, and are not representative of the U.S. Department of Defense. Enjoy the book!"

# PART ONE

# RALDO

—— oOo ——

# CHAPTER 1

# MARCH 2015 – SOMEWHERE IN SOUTH FLORIDA

*Someday, he would look back and the child's reaction to him walking into the restaurant would be funny. At the moment, though, there was not much of anything in which Geraldo Cisneros could find humor.*

*He staggered, hung over, into the bathroom of the 24-hour diner just on the outskirts of the city, and gawked at himself in the mirror.*

*"Monster" was accurate.*

*Raldo had a gash – possibly in need of stitches – just above his left brow, and his right eye was swollen shut. Frankenstein's monster would have cut a more appealing figure, and so Raldo once again had to agree: the small boy who had jumped up in terror, pointed at Raldo as he entered the diner, and practically screamed, "Monster, Mama! Monster!" had made a precise observation.*

*As for the cause of his injuries, who knew? A bar fight? A one-sided assault? Someone throwing him out of a cab or car, after he had turned into a violent drunk? All of it was guesswork.*

*Guesswork was a big part of his life nowadays, particularly during those times when he had sought to piece together the details of the previous night's bender. He had woken up in some strange places after getting wasted, sure, but never in a ditch near a major interstate.*

*There was a first time for everything…as the saying went. That morning marked his first time waking up to the scream of highway traffic just yards from where he had slept.*

*"Like a bum," he could almost hear his father berating him; never mind that the old man had been a world-class drinker in his own right.*

*Raldo ripped a paper towel from the restaurant bathroom's dispenser and ran it under the stream of cold water in the sink. Warm water sounded better at the moment. It was March, but Florida was experiencing an unseasonable cold snap. At that moment, a hot shower sounded divine. Raldo the Marine knew better, though; he had sat through enough Combat Life-Saver Training to know that cold water was preferable. At the moment, he needed vasoconstriction to stop the bleeding, not comfort.*

*He dabbed at the gash on his brow, and remembered his days in the Corps. Since his "end of service" date, alcohol had proven to be a far greater nemesis than any al-Qaeda operative he had ever faced downrange.*

*Raldo looked in the mirror and, for a moment, looked beyond the wounds and the swelling. Instead, he studied his own eyes, but did not recognize them. Staring back at him were two deep voids where his eyes should have been.*

*Nothingness.*

*At that moment, Geraldo Cisneros loathed what he had become.*

*Monster!*

*Was he the monster, or was it the alcohol? Did it really even matter?*

*He glanced down at the frigid water flowing into the dingy basin, and he fought back tears. He had been a warrior, and yet his own demons were kicking his ass. His drinking had cost him his family, and most importantly, his little girl. Reyna would turn nine this year, and Raldo would likely miss her birthday… again.*

*In desperation, Geraldo Cisneros pounded the ceramic sink with his fist, clenched his jaw, and glared at himself in the mirror. Ignoring his ghastly appearance, he focused only on the empty reflection of his eyes, as they continued their languid reflection back at him.*

*"Semper Fi!" he hissed at himself.*

*With that, Raldo walked out of the bathroom and left the restaurant.*

*Five days later, he checked himself into a rehab center in Palm Beach County.*

## DECEMBER 2015

*He didn't want the gig.*

*God, was the entire world out to make him relapse?*

*"Know your triggers, avoid them when you can." Wasn't that the battle cry back at Pleasant Oaks Treatment Center, where he had just graduated from?*

*So how had he, Geraldo Cisneros, been so stupid as to allow himself to get roped into covering a shift for a buddy who worked as a bouncer at a club, of all places?*

*Because the buddy was a former Marine himself, and because they both worked security for a living, that's how.*

*Raldo had to admit that it was a decent break from the bland front lobbies of banks and other tony Palm Beach businesses that he normally worked. And as a freelance security specialist, could he really afford to be choosy?*

*Christmas tunes blared from a jukebox in the corner, and – per usual - the conversation volume rose in proportion to the busy-ness of the bartender, as did Raldo's sense of alert. Naturally, he tried to stay away from bars, mainly because of the alcohol that he had spent six months (successfully) breaking free from, but part of him still loved the clubs; the action, and the knowledge that he was – in some small way – helping folks unwind, perhaps after a busy day or a rough time. Alcohol could be brutal, and no one knew that better than Raldo. But* sometimes folks just needed a drink in peace. And he, Raldo Cisneros, was happy to provide the "peace" part.

If not for the alcohol jones, which he had become aware of even before he hit the barroom floor for that night's shift, Geraldo Cisneros almost felt at home. Things were stable. For the first time in several years, he felt as though he was getting a handle on his life and moving forward in a direction that did not lead to a premature death of some kind.

Best of all, he was setting goals that he felt were actually within reach. He had hit the ground running after being discharged from rehab, and so far had not looked back. That meant no relapses, and aside from the occasional hankering, no genuine desire to get shit-faced anymore. It was a milestone that he had only rarely achieved in his adult life. Come to think of it, he could not remember the last time he had been this consistently sober.

And so, as he stood near the entrance leading to a dark, narrow stairway, which opened into the street above, he scanned the crowd and silently congratulated himself on making it to this point. The next phase for him would be reconnecting with his daughter, but all in good time.

Reyna Evangelina Martita Cisneros.

Raldo thought of her, remembered her, cherished her in his memory.

No matter how drunk he ever got, no matter how much of his memory was wiped out by the alcohol, no amount of it, he was convinced, could ever wipe out the memory of Reyna's *toothy grin. Nothing could sponge away from his conscience the sight of her running toward him with open arms at the age of four, her long, curly brown tresses billowing like a parachute behind her as she catapulted into his waiting embrace.*

*"Te quiero mucho, Papi!" she had exclaimed. "Eres mi heroe!"*

*And Raldo would always return the embrace. After cradling her in his thick arms, he would brush back the hair behind her right ear and "besa la corona," as she always shrieked with delight.*

*"Besa la corona"…"Kiss the crown".*

*The "crown" was a crown-shaped birthmark that he and his ex-wife had noticed shortly after their daughter had been born…after her birth, and not long before Raldo's drinking would wreck everything.*

*That birthmark, crown-shaped and a darker shade than Reyna's brown, Latina skin; Raldo would never forget it. It was how they had named her, in fact; "Reyna"…for "queen" in Spanish.*

*Raldo had kissed that birthmark often, and longed for the day on which he could kiss it once more.*

*Alcohol had robbed him of a place in her life, but it would never take his memory. And if he had anything to say about it, it would not permanently rob him of their future, either. He would win his little girl back. He would make things right.*

*One step at a time. Sobriety was the first step; stable employment was the second; saving money and rebuilding his financial foundation would come next. When the time was right, when he felt that he was finally back in control of things, he would reach out.*

*Saundra, his ex, lived in Miami, and was his only (tenuous) link to Reyna. She had raised the girl on her own since he had exited the picture shortly after returning from Afghanistan in 2012, when his drinking had landed that final crushing blow to their marriage once and for all.*

*Afterward he had spiraled out of control, and wound up at rock-bottom.*

*"Monster!" had been rock-bottom. That snot-nosed little kid in the diner – whose memory Raldo now laughed at - had gotten scared when he saw Raldo's battered face, and mistaken him for something out of a horror film. Little did the boy (or even Raldo) know at that moment, that pronouncement – "Monster" – had actually become the sounding cry for Raldo to turn about; the moment at which he knew he would finally turn from his demons, kick the alcohol once and for all, and embrace what life of his remained, hopefully with Reyna in the picture somewhere.*

*He just had to bide his time.*

*A female voice interrupted his reverie.*

*"Not an easy place to recover from alcoholism, is it?" blurted the chirpy British accent.*

*Raldo started, and turned to see who had paged him.*

*The woman was smiling at him. She was middle-aged, perhaps a few years older than he, and looked about as out of place in a joint like this one as you could get. The bar was an* upper-middle class dive, but this woman looked well above upper-middle class. Attractive, she stood at about five-nine, almost as tall as Raldo, and wore a designer business suit with high heels – definitely not the attire of someone just out for a drink. Her face was thin, but graceful, and it bore the look of someone who knew how to read people.

She chuckled upon seeing his reaction. "Relax, Butch," she told him. "I grew up in a family of alcoholics, so I have a sense about these things."

"Can I help you with something?" Raldo asked her in a dry, professional tone.

"Actually, I'm trying to help you," she told him, taking a seat on a stool near the doorway, where he stood. "I'm Giselle Masterson."

She extended her hand, and he gave her a skeptical glare before slowly accepting it and shaking.

"Prior military?" she asked.

Raldo averted his gaze from her, uncomfortable with the fact that a stranger seemed to know so much about him.

"It shows," she continued, without waiting for an answer. "Guess that's one reason you guys are the best at what you do."

"What do we do?" Raldo inquired.

"Fight, protect, serve," the woman said, with just enough emphasis to make it sound almost mocking.

"Look, I'm kind of busy here, miss," Raldo said, losing patience. "What was it you said you wanted to help me with?"

"I didn't say what I wanted to help you with," she replied.

"At least not yet. Are you interested in listening, or do you want to keep scanning the crowd for unruly office temps?"

Raldo glowered at her.

"Have you ever heard of Carson Pelagius?" she asked.

Raldo thought for a moment, then shook his head.

Giselle nodded, as if his answer was expected. "Lot of folks haven't," she affirmed. "Truth be told, he prefers it that way."

"Who's Carson Pelagius?" Raldo asked.

"A billionaire," she answered. "Financier. A man of influence and power."

Raldo almost laughed. What little Palm Beach lacked in snooty-ass rich folks, it made up for with scam artists. This woman could fit the profile of either.

"What's that got to do with me?" he questioned Giselle.

"Don't be so modest," she flattered. "Stan speaks highly of you."

His eyes narrowed at the mention of the club owner's name. Raldo had covered this bar for his friend on a few occasions, and had even broken up a couple of minor skirmishes. Decent work, but probably not enough to merit a rave review from Stan.

"You've made quite the impression," Giselle followed. "Stan likes your work, and therefore, so do we."

"We?" Raldo questioned.

"Myself and Mr. Pelagius."

Raldo said nothing, and looked away.

Giselle kept her green eyes fixed on him for a moment.

"I wasn't lying when I told you about having a 'nose' for alcoholics because of my family," she said. "But I also know a little about your story from talking to Stan."

Raldo glared at her.

"Relax," she soothed, reading him. "Stan was discreet; didn't offer a lot of details. But he did mention that you were recovering; and he told me about your service in the Marines."

"What do you want from me?" Raldo pressed her.

"To hire you," Giselle said, reaching into the small clutch that she carried. "Private security, exclusively for Mr. Pelagius; for more money per year than what you could make working in this place for the rest of your life."

With that, she pulled a small piece of paper from her purse and handed it to him. It was a business card with a handwritten phone number, and nothing else.

"Think about it," she said. "A tough guy like you can only stay tough for so long in a place that serves alcohol."

With that, she left.

Raldo put the card in his pocket, and tried to forget about the conversation. Snake-oil merchants are everywhere, he thought to himself.

He scanned the barroom and noticed Stan, the owner, coming toward him. He was a squat-heavy man who had taken over the place after serving for years as a bouncer and bartender himself. As he approached, he leaned in so that his hardened, prune-like face was within inches of Raldo's.

"Take the job, kid," he almost snarled, trying to overcome the din of the club.

*Raldo gave him an incredulous look. "What'd you tell that bitch about me, Stan?"*

*Stan glared at him. "Enough to pique her interest in you, you ungrateful prick."*

*Both men held each other's stares for a moment.*

*"Listen," Stan went on, "if you turn down a job from Carson Pelagius, I'll probably fire you myself…then I might kill you. Trust me, Raldo, you're missing the golden opportunity of a lifetime. Don't miss out on it."*

## TWO WEEKS LATER

*"Loyalty," Carson Pelagius almost whispered from behind his mahogany desk in the beachside office of his personal residence. "Loyalty and discretion."*

*Raldo sat across from him, wearing a coat and tie that he had borrowed from someone. Pelagius, for his part, was dressed casually; a short-sleeve white button-down, shirttail out, and khaki pants. On his feet, he wore loafers without socks and appeared as a man who was fully at ease in his own domain.*

*"Do you understand, Raldo?" Pelagius asked, brushing the fingertips of both hands through his thick salt-and-pepper hair. He was in his mid-fifties and had a slight build, but it was clear that he kept himself in decent shape. And he of-*

*ten wore the same expression on his face of detached aloofness combined with a genteel and friendly demeanor.*

*Raldo found his soft-spoken disposition pleasant, and easy to connect with. And yes, for the kind of money he was being offered at this job, he would be more than both loyal and discreet.*

*"I understand," Raldo answered.*

*"I'm glad to hear that," Pelagius said, keeping his eyes fixed on Raldo's. "Now," he gave a mild chuckle, "I know you're probably used to paperwork out the ass in your line of work; not even to speak of what you probably saw when you were in the service. But, I think you'll find that we go by a somewhat simpler code here."*

*"Simpler code?" Raldo asked.*

*"Less paperwork," Pelagius grinned. "Whereas you probably might spend a whole day, or days, signing documents; my operation here is pretty straightforward in that you only have to sign ONE document." He held up a finger and emphasized the word "one".*

*Raldo just nodded, appreciating the sound of this.*

*Pelagius slid a single piece of paper toward him and said, "If you could just sign this one document here, once you've read it of course, we can finalize things and you can begin working."*

*Raldo picked up the sheet and tried to read it. It was definitely shorter, and he relished the idea of having to affix his signature only once instead of over and over again. And yet, as he scanned the legal-ese, he realized that the verbiage was every bit as indecipherable as the crap he'd had to sign at the Marine Corps recruiting station years earlier, never mind the length.*

*The only detail that did make sense to his non-legal mind was the figure at the bottom; his salary.*

*$100,000…after taxes.*

*He glanced up at Pelagius, who met his gaze and smiled, almost as if he could read his mind. "It's real, Raldo," he said. "And all it's basically saying is that you agree, under penalty of litigation, to never disclose what you see inside this residence after we hire you. Confidentiality…total confidentiality. Understood?"*

*"Yeah," Raldo said, his mind still clouded by the six figures.*

*Taking a pen from his shirt pocket, Pelagius handed it to Raldo, who signed his name right away. Pelagius kept a confident smile trained on his new employee the whole time.*

*"Good," Pelagius affirmed, once Raldo had finished. Then, he took up the completed contract with the rapidity with which he had presented it, and was all business again. "Strictly residence duty. And you start today. There's food in the kitchen; charcuterie and shrimp, if you like that stuff." Pelagius then leaned in and whispered, "Personally, I hate fancy stuff, but Giselle loves it, so we have it here."*

*He chuckled and Raldo laughed with him. Just a joke between guys.*

*Fancy or not, Raldo was hungry, and the mention of shrimp, something he had not enjoyed in years, only intensified the empty sensation in his stomach.*

*After shaking hands with Pelagius, he exited the wealthy man's spacious office, and closed the white-painted double doors which opened into the larger sitting area and adjoining kitchen. He was feeling good as he spotted the food sitting on top of a capacious granite countertop, and walked over; carefully, as to avoid bumping into any of the tony furniture and sculptures that dotted the floor plan.*

*Raldo was fixing a plate when a door to another adjoining room off of the kitchen opened and a pretty young girl appeared. Looking at her, Raldo figured she could not have been more than eighteen.*

*She started when she saw him, but then gave him an easy smile.*

*"I didn't mean to scare you," Raldo told her with a smile of his own. "I was just getting some food."*

*"No problem," she answered. "I was looking for Giselle."*

*"Haven't seen her," Raldo responded. "I'm Raldo, by the way," he said, putting down his plate, and extending his hand. "Just got hired to do security."*

*"Charlsy," the girl returned, accepting it in a soft handshake. She seemed in a hurry to leave.*

*Raldo took notice of her immediately. She was dressed in tight jeans that hugged her curves, and a tight low-cut pink top.*

*"You live here?" he asked.*

*"Sometimes," Charlsy answered.*

*Raldo studied her. "Do you work for Mr. Pelagius?"*

*Charlsy hesitated. "You could say that. I want to be an actress, and Carson's helping me get connected with some folks."*

*Raldo nodded, but felt a pang of skepticism. Carson Pelagius, for all his charisma, seemed rather old to be on a first-name basis with a girl that young, who wasn't related to him.*

*"How old are you, Charlsy?"*

*The girl became abrupt and was in a hurry to leave. Turning to walk out the way she came in, she answered, "Eighteen. It was nice to meet you."*

*Raldo just stood there staring at the doors as they closed behind Charlsy.*

*Something about her seemed off.*

## CHAPTER 2
# EARLY 2016

R aldo stood on the balcony of the Pelagius home, cigarette in hand, and stared out into the vast expanse of the Atlantic. As he watched crawly cascades of white wavetops crash against the shore, he thought of whispers.

*Whispered conversations.*

*After several months of working at the Pelagius home, it seemed as though the whispers went hand-in-hand with the opulence and wealth that Raldo saw all around him. And as head of security, he was beginning to master the art of picking up on cues and details and low voices when he patrolled the spacious grounds of the estate.*

*The modern, Spanish-style architectural model was set back about a hundred yards from the shoreline, and offered a majestic view of the ocean. Its multi-story, 48,000-square foot floor plan sat under a Spanish-tile roof and sprawled out on over an acre of land that Carson Pelagius had purchased over a decade ago.*

*Sometimes, he wondered if houses of that size were built so that they could contain all of the secrets within.*

*Things were still good. He was making six figures, and building a new dream, free from want and – as he had originally hoped – on his way to freedom from addiction and a new life with his daughter.*

*And yet, as he sat pondering the latest whispered exchange between Giselle Masterson and Carson Pelagius, he felt the same pangs of skepticism and questioning that he had felt during that first encounter with Charlsy several months earlier.*

*"Her mom gave us permission."*

*"Practically signed the kid's life away."*

*"What would you do in an impoverished situation like that?"*

*"Fourteen years old."*

*Charlsy had been the topic of that conversation, and Raldo now knew that she was fourteen years old…not eighteen, as she had originally said. She came and went from the mansion with such frequency that Raldo had begun to ask questions; always to himself and never out loud.*

*The doorbell interrupted his thoughts, and he immediately snapped into protocol mode. After checking the video monitor sitting on a credenza near the kitchen, he went to the door.*

*"That's Charlsy, with some new friends," Giselle announced, appearing from out of nowhere. She was dressed in*

*a black business suit, similar to the one Raldo had seen her wearing when he had first met her. Her manner was hurried, but not stressed, and she had the demeanor of someone who had a lot to do, but would relish whatever was on the agenda. Her eyes gleamed with a near-surfaced delight, and she busied her hand as she fussed over her hair and outfit, prior to the entrance of the girls at the front door.*

*As was often the case these days, Raldo had questions, but did not dare ask them. Instead, he simply opened the door.*

*"Hey, Raldo," Charlsy said, entering.*

*Behind her were two girls that Raldo had never seen before.*

*"This is Jasmine," she said, pointing to a short, thin girl of about fourteen (maybe even thirteen). Her blonde hair was pulled back into a ponytail, and her dark eyes — like Charlsy's - were deep and sunken, almost hollow. She wore a gray hoodie and tight jeans.*

*"And this is Khaelyn," she said, gesturing to her other companion. Khaelyn was taller, with a thick, almost athletic, frame. Whereas Jasmine looked as though she was a step or two from the streets, Khaelyn looked as though she had just ridden her bicycle to the Pelagius mansion from one of the nearby upper-middle class subdivisions.*

*"I'll need to search you both," Raldo told them, his voice almost robotic.*

*Phones, weapons, and drugs; those were the Big Three. Phones because of the possibility that they may be used to re-*

cord what happened behind the large oak door of the Pelagius house; weapons for obvious reasons; and drugs because… well…they complicated things.

Raldo was thorough but respectful with the girls and soon confirmed that all three were clean. He then led them from the foyer into the large sitting area where Giselle was waiting for them.

"Yes," she began, looking the girls over as an approving smile broke out across the creases of her middle-aged face. "Oh, definitely yes. Charlsy, you've done well. Mr. Pelagius will like these two. Definitely some star potential here."

Charlsy introduced Jasmine and Khaelyn to Giselle. Jasmine seemed taken with the ornate interior of the house, but was noncommittal on Giselle, while Khaelyn's wide-eyed gaping reaction to everything – including Giselle – demonstrated that she was enraptured with all of it.

"Did Charlsy tell you about us?" Giselle pressed the two girls.

"About acting lessons?" Khaelyn spoke up, with enthusiasm.

"Something about college money," Jasmine said, keeping her eyes on Giselle, and studying her.

"Yes," Giselle said in an emphatic, yet measured, tone. "Yes. Mr. Carson Pelagius, as you can already probably tell, is well off and likes to pride himself on having an eye for talent. And he likes to develop said talent, and give opportunities to young ladies like you who might need it."

*The two new girls nodded, accepting this. Charlsy said nothing.*

*"Mr. Pelagius," Giselle went on, "has been looking forward to meeting the both of you, which of course is step number one. Before all of the money starts changing hands, before acting lessons, girls, it's a fact that we must all simply get to know each other." Giselle delivered this last part with emphasis, leaning forward as a teacher would in addressing a group of elementary school students.*

*Raldo felt in his gut a sickening sensation that was recurring all too often nowadays, since...when? Since he had started working for Pelagius? Since he had seen Charlsy – just a few weeks earlier - emerge from Pelagius's bedroom wearing nothing but a long t-shirt? Deep in his viscera, where he always felt sick, he sensed that something was wrong, but fought against having to admit it.*

*He knew about sex trafficking; he knew that teenage girls were at risk for being victims of it; but he had never seen it up close.*

*Was he seeing it up close now?*

*"So," Giselle went on, "without further ado, Mr. Pelagius is waiting. Why don't we therefore head up to his private quarters and spend a little time getting acquainted?"*

*Jasmine and Khaelyn exchanged blank glances, and were soon following Giselle and Charlsy up a marble staircase.*

*As they neared the top, a set of French doors opened, and there stood Carson Pelagius in the doorway. He wore a white shirt, tan Capri pants, and – Raldo thought – the most menacingly lustful smile ever to be worn by a human being.*

*Not long after that encounter was when Raldo had learned the truth.*

*The truth had come to him courtesy of his accidentally walking in during one of Charlsy's "private meetings" with Mr. Pelagius.*

*It was an encounter he would never forget, and one that – despite his years as a marine, and supposedly having "seen it all" – had scarred him in a way that he had never experienced.*

*Shrieks.*

*Charlsy had shrieked as she had scrambled to cover herself, and Pelagius had done practically the same.*

*Raldo had nearly blacked out, and had probably blocked out the details he did not remember, but knew he would remember images of what he had seen on that day for the rest of his life.*

*It was the day he realized that he had sold out in pursuit of a life of freedom and prosperity; no matter how noble his intentions may have been. No matter his desire to reconnect with his daughter, he himself felt vile as he realized the truth.*

*Charlsy was not going to acting school. Nor was Jasmine, nor Khaelyn, nor any of the other dozen or so girls (at least) that had found themselves ensnared in the lair of Mr. Carson Pelagius. They were there for a far more sinister reason.*

*To be sure, Giselle had tried to reassure him otherwise, after she had found him moments later standing on the back porch, nursing a soda, and trying in vain to calm his nerves after seeing the whole incident unfold in Pelagius's bedroom.*

*"It's friendship," she had almost soothed, as they had stood together on the porch. "Charlsy is a friend, Raldo. There was nothing inappropriate about it. Sexual, yes; inappropriate, no; and most certainly all of it was consensual. Charlsy wants to go to acting school; Carson wants to send her. It's like a father-daughter relationship."*

*Raldo had wanted to bash her mealy-mouthed head in right there. Father-daughter relationship?*

*"You sick bitch," is all he managed, panting heavily as he fought to catch his breath.*

*Giselle kept her poise, but hardened her eyes as they bore into him. "So is it back to the bars, then, Raldo? Ruined? Sued? Back to the constant alcohol jonesing? Back to being a washed-out loser? A poor one, at that. Think Stan'll pony up $100,000 a month if you go crawling back to him?"*

*He had no response to this.*

*"I'd recommend reading your contract again. You need us more than we need you."*

*And with that, she'd won. Of course she had, she always did; her and that devil of a man whom she worked for. For them it wasn't the money that defined success. For Carson*

*Pelagius and Giselle Masterson, it was The Hook.*

*The Hook was how influential people succeeded in bending others to their will. Poor people bending to rich people; weak people bending to strong people. It was all the same.*

*Raldo's hook was the money, and the distance between him and the next relapse; the distance between him and his daughter, really. And Giselle had yanked on it like a seasoned fisherman.*

*On cue, and almost as if to drive home the point, Raldo's cell phone had rung as Giselle was leaving the porch for the house.*

*He read the screen. "Saundra."*

*"Yeah?" he answered.*

*"Yeah," came his ex-wife's raspy voice. At one time, Raldo had been attracted to Saundra's bubbly personality and up-beat voice, no matter what it threw at her. In those early days of their courtship, and even their marriage, the world seemed newer and everything seemed possible. They were free as birds, as they had built a life together in whatever place the military had thrown them.*

*Life had gotten the better of their marriage, though; their family, their home all of it. And with that had come Saundra's previously chipper demeanor being eclipsed by a hard cynicism that had infiltrated how she sounded over the phone at that moment.*

*She sounded older, and somehow it scared Raldo.*

*"What is it?"*

*"Heard you were working now."*

*"How'd you hear that?"*

*"Don't play with me, Raldo," she warned. "You know I hear things."*

*"When it comes to my money, I know you do."*

*"Yeah, well, you owe me child support."*

*"You'll get it."*

*"Will I, now?"*

*Raldo's patience was wearing thin. "Why'd you call me, Saundra?"*

*"Who are you working for?" she demanded.*

*"A guy."*

*"Doing what?"*

*"Security."*

*"He rich?"*

*"Maybe."*

*There was a pause. Then: "All right, look. Here's the deal. Your daughter wants to reconnect with you, but I ain't with that. Not yet, anyway. But if your sorry ass can pay me the back child support you owe me, and if you can stay clean, AND stay employed, we can talk about it."*

*Raldo's heart jumped, and he fought against the urge to let his excitement take over his impulses.*

*"How long?" he asked. "Give me a time frame."*

*"One year."*

*Damn,* Raldo thought to himself.

*"Take it or leave it," she almost hissed.*

*"All right, then."*

*"One year to pay your daughter what you owe her, and stay employed, and show me that you ain't gonna relapse; then we'll talk about joint custody again."*

*They hung up. For a moment, he was euphoric, as the realization that his dream of getting to reconcile with his daughter was closer within reach than it had been in years. He grinned as he turned, and felt his mirth shatter almost as quickly as it had arisen. Right then, he realized that he had committed to Carson Pelagius for an entire year.*

*Stay employed; show you ain't gonna relapse, and then we'll talk.*

*Damn that woman. Damn his drinking. Damn Pelagius. And damn the web he was now trapped in. He wanted to see his daughter more than anything else in the world. But in order to do that, he would have to play the game.*

*And so, for that reason, he stayed on. Week after week, month after month, and year after year; always a steady stream of girls entering and exiting the front door. They came in with heads full of big dreams and hearts full of Pelagius-Masterson flattery, and always exited with that same hollowed look that*

*Raldo had first seen in Charlsy's eyes. It was a look of maturity, to be sure, but one borne of hardship, and not the God-ordained milestones set out for young women of age. It was a look of someone whose…what was it? Life? Essence? Youth?… had been sucked out of them by a spider of some kind.*

*A spider named Carson Pelagius.*

*He knew what went on behind those doors now. Since Charlsy, he had not seen any of it first-hand, but he knew. Sometimes, if he dared to listen closely enough, dared to get near to the door, he could hear weeping on the other side, sometimes intermingled with soothing reassurance from Pelagius himself, or Giselle (who sometimes joined in the behind-closed-doors happenings).*

*"It's totally natural," he would hear Giselle's patronizing nasal tone.*

*"Not gonna hurt you, baby girl," Pelagius would mollify.*

*Raldo just stood there; letting it happen, hooked by the money, hooked by the sight of his own daughter running into his arms once more after years of separation.*

*Soon, he began to see the girls as forming a chain; one forged link by link, yard by cursed yard, as the years went by and one right after the other came in – with a friend – and exited, only to return later with a "new friend" for Pelagius to sexually abuse.*

*And when he was finished with them, the afore-arranged plans of fame and fortune (on stage or elsewhere) usually faded with the prospect of Pelagius discarding them like used tissue paper. Raldo never saw them again, and neither Giselle nor Pelagius ever mentioned them.*

*Raldo prayed for his daughter. Prayed that he could one day feel comfortable enough in his own newfound, newly-sober skin to approach her; to be a dad to her again.*

*He prayed that the crap he had seen would wash off. Because what if he did see her again? God, what if the crap he had seen – and been a part of – was somehow visible? Would Reyna see it? Could she one day see it, no matter how hard he had worked at sobriety, at becoming a better person; at becoming the father, for God's sake, that she had always deserved and probably needed? She was ten now; time was running out.*

*He prayed for forgiveness, and that God would somehow not hold back from him the deep, genuine reconciliation and reunion that he so coveted with his daughter, Reyna Angelina Martita Cisneros.*

*He prayed that, somehow, all of the stuff that he had seen and heard – all of the whispers, especially the God-forsaken whispers – would somehow be worth it.*

## Chapter 3

# Over Four Years Later - 2020

*N*erve-numbing. It served him then, and it served him today.

*Marine Corps Martial Arts (or MCMAP) had been one of the more enjoyable elements of his time spent serving his country. Raldo had always been a fighter; hell, the more drunk he had been, the better he'd fought. And so when the opportunity to learn fighting had come along – even if it was a somewhat different style than the barroom brawling he was used to – Raldo had jumped at the chance.*

*First, though, came nerve-numbing.*

*Raldo remembered standing in front of a camouflage-clad partner, who had proceeded to hit him repeatedly in the gut, each blow landing directly on his solar plexus nerve, just above the navel and right beneath his rib cage. It hurt like hell, but wasn't that the point? Getting that particular nerve as desensitized to pain as possible was the first step in mastering MCMAP.*

*And so Raldo had persevered. He had come to appreciate the nerve-numbing blows to his gut as only a fighter can learn to appreciate pain. Truth was, he had even begun to get a degree of enjoyment out of the exercise, as he prepared to fight hand-to-hand with God-only-knew-who.*

*And as he stood once more in his favorite location on Pelagius's balcony, once more smoking a Marlboro and gazing out on the Atlantic horizon, he congratulated himself on persevering again at this point.*

*Nerve-numbing; that was the point; the antidote.*

*His nerves were numb today, but those of a different set. He now recognized that his nerves could withstand the realities that had encircled him for over four years now (Jesus, had it been that long?). He no longer winced at the sound of the doorbell, no longer felt an impending sense of dread when he opened the front door to see a doe-eyed girl standing there, entirely unaware of what was getting ready to happen to her at the hands of Carson Pelagius. He no longer felt that deep pity as he caught wind of whatever this new girl's dream was, fully cognizant of the fact that her dream was just about to be smashed to bits. Smashed in a manner far exceeding any Greek tragedy he'd ever heard of.*

*He made his rounds, he did his duty, he collected his paycheck.*

*And over time, he even got used to the sound of weeping coming from that God-forsaken back bedroom.*

*He got used to the stories; how Giselle and Pelagius would come across a girl at a park; how Pelagius would point her out; how Giselle would strike up a conversation and soon confirm the same, tragic story over and over again; poor girl, broken home, big dreams, ready to leap at the chance of money and acting lessons, and fortune, and all of it.*

*He heard the stories, and was almost immune to it.*

*Immune? Raldo almost laughed at his own word choice.*

*Nobody was immune in 2020.*

*That new virus that had originated in Wuhan, China and had made its way all over the globe was wreaking havoc; all except for within the Pelagius mansion, it seemed.*

*It was almost a predictable cliché, but rich people everywhere seemed to be exempt from the "COVID rules", as they were called.*

*And so Carson and Giselle's business went on as usual, and the girls kept right on coming. The boss had a type – an age, really - and that age-type was always available, COVID be damned. Giselle prowled the nether regions of Palm Beach, Broward, and Dade counties like a panther. And she always delivered: black, brown, and blonde hair; any hair color, really. And body types of all kinds as well.*

*For Raldo's part, he kept his head down and dreamed about Reyna.*

*Since his and Saundra's first unpleasant conversation, he had kept up sporadic contact with her, mainly to keep her apprised of how his "year" was going. Of course, per usual, she had used her otherworldly skill at manipulation and had managed to stretch his required "year" into four now. Raldo was pissed, but there was nothing he could do. She held the upper hand, and was content to keep getting regular child support, no matter how sincerely he conveyed his desire to see Reyna and foster a new relationship.*

*Occasionally, Pelagius himself would remind Raldo, sternly but amicably, that "loyalty was the word," and that he was "contract-bound" to keep silent; to which Raldo never balked, never indicated any push-back, nothing. His was a job of discretion and care. And he would do it…for the money, and for his daughter.*

*And so, loyal he would be, and silent. He had no choice but to trust his employers, keep working, keep staying sober, keep making money, and keep reaching out to Reyna with as much good faith as he could muster. Eventually, it would all pan out, and they could be together.*

*She was fourteen now, and Raldo often wondered if she would even recognize him if they saw each other again.*

*"Raldo?" came the voice that interrupted his thoughts.*

*He turned and saw Giselle approaching him. Today, she was dressed in a white shirt and blue jeans.*

*No new girl today, he assumed. Giselle only got dressed up on days when they were expecting new "talent", which was the perverse moniker they used.*

*"Carson's closing out a big deal in Manhattan over the internet," she informed him, coming forward and stuffing her hands into her back pockets. "No one's cooking. Can you call and order pizza?"*

*Raldo grinned. He had come to be somewhat amazed at the often simple tastes enjoyed by Pelagius and Giselle. As a power couple, they enjoyed their fair share of fine dining. And yet, at the same time, Raldo had been dispatched on many occasions to Stuffy's Pizza on the other side of town for whatever they were in the mood for that night.*

*"Sure."*

*"The usual," she instructed, as she left the room again. "White cheese for me, and you know Carson; meat-lovers. Can't get enough meat, that guy."*

*No, he can't, Raldo said to himself. It sounded like a joke, but Raldo felt dirty for even thinking it. Jesus, had he really become this desensitized?*

*He grabbed a pen and paper from the credenza in the kitchen, and was jotting down the pizza order details when the doorbell rang.*

*Raldo made his way to the door, and racked his brain as he tried to think of appointments and visitors that he may have overlooked. It was nearly six in the evening, and while visitors at that hour were not unheard of, Pelagius usually had things wrapped up at the house (business meetings, girls, etc.) by no later than four. Surprises were never a good thing when you were Carson Pelagius…or when you worked for him, for that matter.*

*He reached the door and glanced through the specially-designed sight apparatus, which was more than just a peephole. It gave him (and anyone who looked through it) a clear, non-distorted view of whoever was on the doorstep.*

*It was Madison, one of the newer girls. Why was she here?*

*Madison stood in front of the door wearing a yellow halter top and tight jeans. Her straight, shoulder-length blonde hair cascaded to her shoulders, and her eye shadow was doing its best to conceal that all-too-common hollowness of the eyes that Raldo barely noticed anymore.*

*Tonight, though, there was someone else with her – another girl - whom Raldo did not recognize, and who was too far back in the porch light shadows for him to see clearly.*

*Positive ID of everyone; that had been the standing order given to him by both Pelagius and Giselle on numerous occasions. He could not take chances, no matter how innocuous this new girl looked.*

*Even before that, though, he needed to verify the visit.*

*"What is it, Maddy?" he called out through the door.*

*"Carson wants to see us," she answered, her tone almost insistent.*

*"Shit, I'm sorry, Raldo," came Giselle's voice, as she bounced once more into the spacious kitchen and sitting area. "I just remembered that Carson did make a late-evening appointment with a new girl. Maddy's just bringing her by. So sorry, I completely forgot. Let's get her in here, and then you can go get the pizzas."*

*Raldo nodded, turned back to the door, and addressed Maddy. "That's fine, but I still need to make a positive ID. Have her step forward so I can see her."*

*Maddy turned and gave a slight gesture with her head,*

*which cued the new girl to step forward into the porch light. She was wearing jeans and a gray hoodie, which concealed her hair and part of her face.*

*"Take the hood off," Raldo commanded, keeping his eye glued to the viewer.*

*The girl complied, and as she took down her hood, Raldo took note of her Hispanic-looking features. Everything about her seemed dark, and yet – of course - somehow innocent.*

*He unlocked the door, satisfied that things were on the up-and-up. As the door swung inward, Maddy entered first, followed by her new friend. She passed Raldo without looking at him, and as she did, Raldo caught the faintest whiff of something that he knew, but could not put his finger upon. It was a scent that caused his memory to stir. Why was he thinking of his honeymoon with his ex-wife all of a sudden?*

*Again, he had to snap himself out of it, and re-focus on his duties.*

*He frisked Maddy in the same professional manner in which he had frisked dozens of girls (as well as businessmen and other acquaintances of Mr. Pelagius) over the years. Then he moved on to the new girl.*

*After giving her a brief pat-down, he rose to eye level with her and, for the first time, made eye contact.*

*She was new, all right. Her brown eyes betrayed a vague wariness about why she was there, who she was about to meet, what was about to happen to her, and what it all might mean for her future. And yet, in her eyes there was also a seamless intermingling of innocence that went right along with the uncertainty.*

*She also looked familiar somehow.*

*"This is Rae," Maddy told him, in a cockeyed, clumsy effort to be cordial and well-mannered.*

*"Hi," Raldo said to Rae, who managed to return the greeting.*

*The smell of that perfume, and something about that girl.*

*Giselle entered and broke his train of thought with a chirpy, "Mr. Pelagius is in his room, and is ready to see you both. And I think he's going to love you, Rae."*

*Rae returned the flattery with a slight grin.*

*Maddy turned to go first, followed by Rae, who barely regarded Raldo as she passed. Raldo averted his eyes from her just as she was turning, making his way to the door to head for the pizza parlor.*

*No...you've got to go back...get a second look...you saw something! What was it?*

*Raldo had no idea what his subconscious was doing to him now, but God...had he really seen something? And what was it? And why was he almost being pulled by some invisible force to go back and look at this strange girl who had just entered his world.*

*He put together a farce on the spot, and acted like he was missing his car keys. He made for the door to the bedroom-office where Mr. Pelagius was, and which led to the back patio where he had enjoyed his quiet time earlier before being dispatched for pizza.*

*Giselle was standing near the door, and gave him a quizzical look as he approached, both of them knowing that he had no business in the bedroom when Mr. Pelagius was "entertaining".*

*"Car keys," he indicated to her, and kept moving closer to where the girls were preparing to enter. "Think I may have left them on the patio."*

*As Raldo neared Rae, he kept his hands his pockets, pretending to fumble around, while keeping one eye on this new — and strangely familiar - girl.*

*What was it about her? What had he caught a glimpse of as she had turned to leave his presence?*

*His eyes fell upon the spot just behind her right ear, and he had to stifle a gasp.*

*A crown-shaped birthmark was directly behind it.*

*Raldo almost fainted as he suddenly realized who the new girl was.*

# Part Two

# CHAPS

oOo

### Chapter 4

# North Charleston, South Carolina – Summer 2020

Chaplain Whit Gregg sat in his office and looked across the desk at Seaman Rose Hartman, but did not really see her. Instead, he saw his daughters.

After what she had just told him, he felt nauseous; along with the impulse of possibly losing his temper. He fought to restrain the rage that percolated within him, fully aware that anything rash could very well result in him losing his commission as an officer and a chaplain in the United States Navy.

So he kept his eyes on the young woman in front of him. She was barely nineteen and had just joined the Navy, likely as a means to better herself, and was now going through training at Whit's command; the Naval Nuclear Power Training Site in Charleston – also known shorthand as "the Site".

Rose's ruddy complexion, combined with the tears she wept, caused splotches of red to gather around her eyes. Whit offered her a tissue, which she accepted as she began dabbing at them. This was followed by a pitiful nose-trumpeting as she blew out snot and, Whit hoped - whimsical as it seemed - as much of the negativity and angst that she was feeling as was possible.

He gave her a moment to gather herself. These strategic pauses were helpful in just about every counseling session Whit had ever been a part of, whether as a Navy chaplain or anywhere else in professional ministry. Severe distress often called for prolonged silence before anything else was said.

When she had calmed, Whit pressed – ever so gently – once more. "So, without making you more upset, Rose, can you just tell me again, just so I'm clear, what it was that Captain Bestgen said to you?"

Rose drew in a deep breath, then she answered, "He told me I was no better than a rapist or sexual predator."

The words pierced Whit's mind like shards of glass.

It was a new low even for Captain Andrew Bestgen, the commander of the Nuclear Power Training Site. Whit was reminded once more of why he often referred to his boss as "Worst-gen" under his breath and behind the mask he was now required to wear.

"He compared you to a sexual predator, because…"

"Because I went to Folly Beach and spent the weekend with my boyfriend at his beach house."

"And because you did so in violation of his COVID restriction mandate."

Rose nodded.

At the Site, good days were hard to come by as it was. You showed up to work expecting to feel like garbage by the time the day was finished. Whit had experienced it in spades since he had checked in about midway through 2019.

Then 2020 started. Soon thereafter, COVID-19 made its presence felt, and the spiritual degradation surrounding Chaplain Whit Gregg had only intensified from there. And right in the middle of it, there he was; expected to provide spiritual support and do everything to make sure morale among his fellow sailors did not entirely vanish.

*A sexual predator*, Whit thought to himself, still trying to remain even-keeled. *For going to a beach house.*

His anger burned.

*Breathe, dammit,* he commanded himself. *Keep it together. Help me, Jesus.*

"Look at me," he instructed Rose in a soft voice.

Rose lowered the tissue from her face, and trained her red-splotched eyes on him.

"You," he began in as gentle a tone as he could muster, "are not what Captain Bestgen said you are. Do you understand?"

Rose nodded.

"Say it," Whit said. "Say it out loud."

Rose's chest was still choked with intermittent, hiccup-like sobs, but she managed to find a break in them and reply with, "I am not what he said I am."

"Whatever mistakes you may have made by going to that beach house," Whit continued, "that does not make you a bad person. And it sure to God does not make you anywhere near comparable to a sexual predator. Do you understand?"

Rose nodded and squeaked out a faint, "Yes."

"You are God's creation, and you matter to Him. Do you understand?"

Again, she affirmed with a nod.

"Do you believe me?"

"Yes."

"Good."

Rose gave him a faint smile.

"Will you remember something else?"

Rose gave a slight nod.

"Things are going to work out," Whit told her. "I don't know how, but they will. Just trust what I say…and trust God, if you can."

They were silent for another moment, while Rose's tears continued. When they had subsided, Whit asked, "Are you in an okay place now?"

Rose nodded.

"Good."

They parted ways after a few more moments, and after

Whit had – with Rose's permission – said a short prayer with her. He also made her promise to come and see him again if she needed to. Of course, both of them knew that they would see each other again when Rose finally went to Captain's Mast – her punishment for going to the beach house and breaking the Captain's rules.

Whit dreaded it – for her – and wondered if his feeling was somewhere close to how strongly Rose had to have been feeling about it.

Either way, it was coming, and just the thought of it caused Whit's pulse to race. *Empathy has a price*, he thought to himself, as he fought to steady his heartbeat.

Anger soon took the place of trepidation as Whit sat in his office chair listening to the buzzing of the hallway just outside of his office. The Site's main building was bustling with students, all of whom were training for careers as nuclear reactor operators in the Navy.

Whit sat at his desk and glanced across it. Ever the neat-freak, his one vice in this area was his desk. He often chuckled at how he allowed it to clutter against his usual impulse to keep things in order.

Today, however, he was far from any sort of laughter. As he scanned the moderate amount of desk debris, his eyes came to a particular piece of paper that had been sitting there for some time.

Whit picked it up, and noticed that it was a letter of commendation that Worst-gen had given him some time ago, after Whit had volunteered to provide the opening and closing prayers for a ceremony out in town. *Give the bastard his due credit,* Whit thought to himself, as he considered his previous commanding officers, many of whom had never shown Whit any discernible appreciation for his efforts as the chaplain of their units. *Worst-gen knows how to throw you a bone every once in a while.*

He studied the letter, which was rife with flattery.

*Lieutenant Gregg,*

*I want to personally thank you for…Your efforts have proven to be a credit to the Navy once more…You are to be commended for…*and so forth.

As Whit read over the words, he felt an old familiar warmth rising to the surface of his heart; the kind born only of legitimate affirmation and praise for one's efforts and contributions. Whit had known his own heart's love of flattery for years, but was determined now – more than ever – to resist it.

At that moment, he pictured Rose's tear-splotched face, her sobs, and – worst of all – her likeness to his own daughters. She was sensitive, feminine, and almost child-like; all of which summoned forth the same protective instinct within Whit that he recognized when it came to Ava (age seven) and Esther (age four).

And so, at that moment, as he held the commendation letter in his hand, he wanted to beat the ever-loving shit out of Andrew Bestgen.

Instead, he tore the paper in half; then again, and again, and over and over until his hands were filled with little snowflake-like specks of discarded letter…discarded affirmation and flattery…which Whit drizzled into his office garbage can.

Chaplain Whit Gregg then sat back in his chair, covered his face with his hands, and sighed heavily. "Help me, Jesus."

# CHAPTER 5

Driving home in the evening was typically a golden opportunity for Whit to unwind and unload the stress of the day. Sometimes it involved music, and at other times destressing was as simple as rolling down his driver's side window and letting the cool South Carolina evening breeze whittle away the day's cares.

These were not typical days, though.

These days, students like Rose Hartman lingered in Whit's mind, as he navigated the decaying, congested streets of north Charleston. These days, he found himself consumed with a deeper anger.

Since the onset of the COVID pandemic, Whit had worn his mask indoors; he had maintained social distance wherever and whenever possible, and he had ensured that his family largely did the same. He had even gone so far on a few occasions as to *encourage others* to do the same. To his mind, those elements came easy, especially the social distancing part. Whit hated large crowds, did not generally enjoy people infiltrating his personal space (or that of his family members), and tried to be respectful of the "bubbles" of everyone around him.

But lockdowns? Restrictions outside of work? Treating people as though they were dumb animals? Whit had seen it all in the past several months. He'd seen it in the news, heard about it via social media, and if that was not enough, had been given a front row seat to the impact it was having on the men and women who wore the same uniform that he did.

Rose Hartman was a classic example. Was it the right thing for her to spend the weekend with her boyfriend at the beach? Probably not. But…

*Sexual fucking predator*, he kept whispering to himself.

He loathed his commander, and despised the military brass and politicians who made decisions far above his pay grade.

It was incidents like these that had left him with serious doubts as to whether or not he could continue on as a chaplain in the Navy…certainly on active duty. Truth was, that aspect of Whit's life had been in flux for a while now, with or without the angst he felt. As a chaplain in the rank of Lieutenant, he had already been passed over for promotion to the next pay grade three times. Ordinarily, that was grounds for automatic separation from the Navy, but Whit had been "fortunate" (if that was even the right word) to be granted an extension on active duty. In truth it was fortunate, he always concluded during these moments of wavering, since it allowed him to stay in and provide for his family for the time being.

Whit's mind mirrored the dense fog that was rolling in as he pulled into the parking lot of the apartment complex, where he shared a two-bedroom unit with Rachel and their two daughters. It was a temporary home; one they would live in until they moved again, likely back down south where they owned a house and some acreage in the Florida panhandle. If Whit got off of active duty within the year – a plan which was looking more and more likely by the day – then Florida would be their next destination. He missed it; and moreover, he knew that his family missed their "forever home" (as the girls called it).

Whit parked the car in the dingy lot, and killed the engine. Climbing out, he grabbed the bags he took with him to work each day, and headed inside.

The girls were already asleep – it was a school night – and so Whit was careful to enter quietly. The apartment was unusually still and silent as he made his way into the small foyer and started back toward his and Rachel's master bedroom.

His wife of almost ten years was sitting on the bed, and appeared to be alternating between looking at her iPad and poring over an assortment of notepads that were strewn about the area where she sat.

*Bible study or budget?* Whit mused as he entered and gave her a tired wink and smile. The girls, the budget, the household, errands, you name it – Rachel did it all. And Whit loved her for it.

"How was your day?" she asked, making every effort to multi-task between household manager and loving wife.

Whit made no verbal response, but managed a low, guttural response which – after almost a decade of marriage – Rachel recognized right away.

"That good, huh?" she studied him.

Whit, still in uniform, put his satchel on the ground next to his dresser, doffed his camouflage blouse, and descended to the spot on the bed next to her. He kept his boots on, and rubbed his eyes with the balls of his wrists.

"Do you want to talk about it?" she asked him.

"Only if you want to hear the same story again."

"I'm sorry," she soothed.

Whit acknowledged her with his eyes. "End of active service date cannot come fast enough," he said, surprising himself with the words.

She nodded and regarded him gently. As a couple, they agreed on most things, and even saw eye-to-eye on his departing active duty soon. Their agreement, however, did not change the fact that it would still be a financial leap of faith. Both of them knew that Rachel would have to leave behind the stay-at-home mom life which she had enjoyed since the birth of their daughters, and return to a career of some kind – likely as a nurse. Her reticence about this notwithstanding, she also had a soft spot for her husband's predicament, his unhappiness and lack of fulfillment in his current career. And for this reason, she had never balked – at least not openly - when Whit had first suggested the idea of leaving the Navy for a career teaching high school English.

"Any problems with Bestgen today?"

"Worst-gen, you mean?" Whit rejoined.

Rachel shot him a mild, disapproving glance. *Be nice, be respectful, but I understand* was the unspoken message.

"He compared a nineteen-year-old female student to a sexual predator just for going to the beach during CO-VID."

"What?" Rachel was mortified.

Without naming names, Whit then told her about the exchange with Seaman Rose Hartman.

Rachel shook her head. "Did you say anything to him?"

Whit snorted. "Are you kidding?"

It was all she needed to hear. Andrew Bestgen had made it clear to Whit from day one just how little regard he had for either religion or the advisement from a reli-gious figure, especially a chaplain. On his first day at the Site, Whit had every expectation of having a short sit-down with his new commanding officer; the same kind of short, ten-minute conversation he'd had with every other commander he had worked for. And yet, Andrew Bestgen had given him a head-nod and grunted "welcome" when

Whit had been introduced by his predecessor at the first morning meeting. It was an unusual greeting, but Whit had laughed it off; the same way he often laughed off red flags when it came to disdainful people he met. It was something he hated about himself.

"I'm sorry, babe," Rachel soothed.

"Me too," he said, putting his arms around her and snuggling against her.

Moments passed.

"Are you hungry?" she asked, with a familiar softness in her voice that caused him to perk up.

"A little," Whit answered with a smile.

"There's chicken," Rachel added, cutting her eyes at him with a seductiveness that he recognized.

"Any breasts or thighs?" Whit asked, drawing a chuckle from his wife.

"Maybe," she said, rubbing his chest. "Are those your favorites?"

He nodded. "Always the most enjoyable parts."

They leaned in and kissed, and were soon making love with the lights on.

Afterward, Whit threw on a pair of shorts and a t-shirt and walked back to the small bedroom that was shared by both of his daughters.

Per usual, he maneuvered the door knob off its latch and pushed it open, seeking to minimize the amount of noise he made as he entered.

Rachel's love had cheered him up; at least for the moment. And staring at the cherubic faces and heads of Ava and Esther while they slept heightened the euphoria even more.

Whit studied his daughters as they lay in their beds, and chuckled once more at how virtually everything about them – including how they slept – showcased their night-and-day different personalities.

Ava, his oldest, slept under her covers in a tight bundle, with her blonde hair strewn out over her pink and white pillow. Her prone posture on the bed was as prim and ladylike as it was at just about every moment during which she was awake.

Then there was Esther. She lay on top of her covers and was never bundled. Rather, each of her four limbs were splayed in different directions, almost as if she were directing the tooth fairy or another celestial being who administered dreams.

*It's worth it,* he told himself as he stood in the center of the messy room and watched his daughters sleeping. *Worst-gen, his bullshit, the COVID bullshit flowing south to Charleston from Washington, DC. All of it.*

At that moment, the tiny, cramped room where his girls slumbered was not just their bedroom, but a sanctuary for himself. It was a safe place from the cares that Whit shouldered on a daily basis. And yet, it was also so much more than that. Whit stood there watching their innocence in repose, and felt as though God Himself was providing an ever-so-gentle reminder about why he was where he was. Whit knew that he would relish the day when he no longer had to wear the uniform and put up with all of the detritus that came with his job, but for the moment, he wanted to do it if for no other reason than to give his girls the kind of life where they might hopefully steer clear of the Andrew Bestgens of the world.

And so he kissed his daughters good-night and headed out once more into the living room. It was conjoined with the kitchen and dining area in such a way that provided a modicum of comfort, even though their apartment's floor plan was a fraction of the size of their spacious home back in Florida.

In the small dining area, on their dinner table, sat a plate of chicken that Rachel had set out after Whit had left their bedroom to say good-night to the girls. Whit chuckled mildly as he glanced at it, remembering the innuendo that had led to their lovemaking earlier.

Whit sat down to eat, and Rachel soon joined him from the kitchen, where she had been fixing herself a cup of decaf.

He smiled as she sat down, and noticed right away that the smile she returned was almost forced.

Rachel placed her cup on the table and stared at him for a moment. "Have you thought more about what we discussed?"

Whit's eyes met hers, and he knew exactly what she was talking about. It was a conversation that he did not want to have, especially tonight, but which he also knew needed to happen.

"About counseling?"

"Yeah."

"I've thought about it," he told her.

"And?"

"And," Whit began, still unsure of what he wanted to say, and even less certain of how he should say it. "And I don't know."

Rachel's eyes narrowed as she continued to study her husband. "Is that a genuine 'I don't know', or a get-out-of-the-conversation 'I don't know'?"

Whit almost chuckled. He knew the answer and, even worse, so did Rachel.

"Guess if I'm being honest, I don't want to do it," he almost blurted.

"Because?"

"Because I don't like the idea of talking to someone about my problems."

Rachel lowered her eyes for the first time. It was a bullshit answer, and both of them knew it; especially Whit.

Rachel seemed to read his mind. "'It's more shameful

to let your demons win than to admit that you need to face them.'" She parroted this line, which she'd heard uttered by Whit dozens of times in her presence – in church pulpits, in talking in front of sailors and spouses, everywhere – as a mockery against his obstinance.

Whit's defenses were crumbling as they sat together at the kitchen table. "I just…" he began.

"You just hate how things are," she said.

Whit wanted to crawl under the table, and escape the blue eyes of his wife that had the power – since the early days of their courtship and engagement – to level him with only a glance. He despised this feeling of vulnerability; despised it and loved it all at once.

Rachel sensed it, and reached for his hand. Taking it in hers, she said, as if soothing a child, "It's okay, Whit."

Whit felt hot tears coming to his eyes, as the detritus of the day seemed to well up within his soul.

"You don't have to tackle everything alone," she stated. "This Dr. Allenby is a solid guy; everyone I've talked to at church says he's the best in his field. And every review I've read is off the charts. You owe this to yourself."

Whit looked up at his wife, and wondered if his eyes had the same red splotches which he had seen dotting the face of Rose Hartman only hours earlier.

He sighed after a long moment.

"Give me his number."

# Chapter 6

Whit closed his eyes in desperation, and tried to focus on a single thought.

Then he tried to pray; something that was becoming harder and harder to do lately, no matter how hard he tried. His relationship with God, stalwart as it was, seemed to be changing, and his prayers seemed more and more like calling out to someone in the midst of a noisy party.

God was there, but could he hear?

Thankfully, Rachel was also there, and she could definitely hear.

She had been the one who had gone online and looked up Nature Vista Counseling Services Center, which was located not too far from their home. And she had also been the one who had put her foot down and insisted that he go there and get help. As Whit replayed the conversation in his head, he found himself thanking God for his bride of almost ten years. It was about the only aspect of his prayer life that actually came easily these days.

*I'm not going to be a widow and a single parent, buddy.*

If her sturdy, feminine voice didn't get the message across, her tenacious, tired eyes definitely did.

Whit had never entertained the thought of suicide, but Rachel was not taking any chances. His depression seemed to be intensifying, and she was not going to lose him, Nor were her girls going to lose a father if she had anything to say about it.

So here he was.

What was the guy's name again?...

Whit pulled out of his pocket the printout that Rachel had given him before he'd kissed her and the girls that morning on his way out….

Dr. Cloyce Allenby

Whit took a deep breath.

More and more, it seemed that breathing was the only thing standing between him and a total emotional and spiritual meltdown. The contempt he felt was almost suffocating at times; contempt that he felt for his commanding officer and many other people since COVID had made its big appearance. His anger – a problem before early 2020 – had now seemed to take on new life of its own; to the extent that Whit had become skilled in the practice of "thought interruption".

*Jesus, help me…*Whit barely whispered through the cloth mask that seemed to choke his face.

"Whit Gregg?" a warm voice belonging to an older

man chimed, interrupting the depraved thoughts coursing through Whit's troubled mind.

Dr. Cloyce Allenby, the owner of the warm voice, was in his late sixties. He was a balding man whose well-cropped shocks of gray hair gracefully circled the sides of his head, and which complemented his business casual attire; a robin's egg-blue shirt with a deeper-blue tie and tan slacks.

Whit stood, and was greeted by Dr. Allenby with a firm handshake and a kind smile that put Whit more in mind of a grandfather figure than of a Ph.D. in Christian counseling.

Whit returned the greeting and followed him into a spacious yet modest office. There was a well-appointed desk in one corner near a window that looked out on the Center's parking lot. Cata-cornered to it, on the other side of the room, was a small, faux-leather sofa with an even smaller coffee table in front of it, as well as a matching chair directly across.

As a chaplain, whose job was largely characterized by counseling, Whit understood - and admired - the significance of the set-up.

*Administration in one corner, Real Work in the other.*
*Counseling is the art of getting people comfortable enough*

*to say out loud what they already know. A counselor's job is to simply "grease the skids" in getting them to the point where they do just that.* Whit remembered the words of a sagacious seminary professor he had once studied under.

Dr. Allenby gestured, and Whit took a seat on the sofa.

*Role reversal*, he mused as he sat down.

Dr. Allenby eased himself into the chair across the table from Whit.

"So," he began, "a Navy chaplain."

Whit nodded. "Yes, sir. That's correct."

Allenby grinned an even larger grin. "I was a Navy corpsman myself before I got out and went to seminary. You know what that means, right?"

Whit studied him for a moment.

"It means, you don't have to call me 'sir', Allenby concluded. "I worked for a living in the Navy."

Whit managed a slight chuckle at the age-old joke that was continually bandied about between enlisted personnel and commissioned officers. For some, calling an enlisted man or woman "sir" or "ma'am" was akin to commenting on their weight or sexual preference.

"Sorry," Whit rejoined. "Old habit; dates back to before the Navy, even."

"Where are you from?" Dr. Allenby asked, interested.

"Florida panhandle," Whit answered.

"L.A.," Dr. Allenby replied. "Lower Alabama."

Whit laughed again, with a bit more heartiness this time.

Dr. Allenby continued, "I spent some time in that area for training during my days as an enlisted man," he said, his spry eyes lighting up at the memory.

Whit wondered for a moment if this "counseling session" was about to turn into another "veteran run-in"; the kind he dreaded each time an old guy with a "Vietnam Veteran" ball cap approached him while he was in uniform and proceeded to regale him with "sea stories" filled with indecipherable terms which never made any sense to Whit. He hoped that this wasn't the case with Dr. Allenby, and that he also wouldn't waste the dollars he was getting courtesy of Whit's insurance in talking about his own military experiences.

After all, Whit was here to talk about himself. *Who takes care of the chaplain?* was a common refrain. Well, here he was. *Let's get help.*

"But enough about me," Allenby said, seeming to read Whit's mind as he focused his kind eyes on him. "We can talk about my military experience, and southern traditions, and calling people 'sir' by habit anytime we want." He adjusted in the leather chair, creating a slight leathery rumble as he moved, and seemed to focus on Whit even more intently.

"Tell me about you," he said, crossing one leg over the other, and folding both of his hands in his lap.

Dr. Allenby kept his smiling gaze on Whit, who took a deep breath as he began.

Lieutenant Whit Gregg had entered active duty with the Navy as a chaplain in the spring of 2010. By that summer, he had reported to his first command – Marine Corps Base Camp Pendleton - and was already in work-ups for a deployment to Afghanistan, which took place the following November. During that time, he and Rachel had married, and so Whit had found himself acclimating to married life in the midst of preparing to go to a foreign place of battle halfway around the globe and be the spiritual caregiver to a group of warriors who had more experience on fields of battle than Whit ever would.

Looking back, certainly on paper, the odds had been stacked against him from the word "go". Whit had struggled to establish any meaningful credibility with the troops, regardless of how many ruck marches, PT sessions, or field trainings he had attended. Whit had even (eagerly) volunteered to accompany the platoons to the rifle range and had unofficially qualified as a sharpshooter.

None of it had mattered. He was still the greenhorn of the unit. Minus the credibility, he may as well have not been there.

And thus had begun a ten-plus year career that had seen more instances of disappointment than victories.

In all fairness, his next assignment had been somewhat more fruitful; this one taking him and Rachel (now pregnant with Ava) to Virginia Beach. The atmosphere among the Naval aviators with whom Whit now found himself working was far more laid back and relaxed than the Marine units had ever been, and Whit saw it as a fresh start to his professional life. Everyone was happy to have him around, and Whit enjoyed their company as well.

Then the next deployment happened; this one on an aircraft carrier, and brought with it its own share of frustrations and challenges. Whit found himself in the middle of squabbles between the ship's company (those naval personnel who were organically assigned to the ship) and Whit's unit, who had attached to the ship in support of the upcoming tour. To say that there was a lack of cohesiveness between his air wing and the ship's company was an understatement. Whit heard constant griping and discontentment from his unit, and was inclined to sympathy. Here they were, supposed to be focused primarily on flying missions and maintaining aircraft, and yet, to the ship, it was as if they had inherited a maid service. There was constant pressure on Whit's unit to "loan" their aircraft maintainers for working and clean-up parties of various kinds – which cost them in terms of manpower and man hours that could have been spent taking care of the aircraft responsible for executing missions. All of it led to rifts that Whit felt powerless to maintain.

*Powerless*; a recurring, sordid theme in Whit's career.

Then there was the ill treatment that came at the hands

of senior ship's company officers. Whit himself, on one occasion, had been berated by the ship's supply officer for wearing PT shorts and a t-shirt in the wardroom. When Whit (politely) brought up the fact that another senior officer had done essentially the same thing, he was dismissed harshly and ended up being scolded a second time by his own executive officer. At other times, Whit had expressed frustration at not getting the kind of support to do his job that he needed. Other people were screwing up, and yet Whit was the bad guy for daring to say something about it.

As good as Whit had felt about his second tour, all of these run-ins had cost him on his latest fitness report, which had in turn taken their professional toll on him when he had come up for promotion to the rank of Lieutenant Commander. And as a result, he had spent his entire third tour (at a small shore command in Panama City Beach, Florida) languishing as he fell behind other chaplains whom he knew and had trained with prior to entering active duty. They had almost all promoted, while he remained a married, Lieutenant father of two kids (Rachel had since given birth to Esther, their second) and was now facing having to get out due to failing to select for promotion.

He was now on his fourth (and likely final) active-duty tour at NNPTS in Charleston, South Carolina, and these days he found himself wondering what it was all for.

Why had he seemingly wasted his time – his life, his energy, all of it – doing what he had done?

On top of it all, the world was in the grip of the COVID-19 panic, and none moreso than the U.S. military.

Whit had watched helplessly as his own commanding officer had stated – loudly and brazenly – that he wanted his staff members to be "Big Brother" and crack down on anyone they saw not wearing a mask, wanting to exit the training base for any reason, and come within the prescribed safe distance of six feet of each other. Questions were to be asked, "MAINTAIN SIX FEET!" was to be bellowed, and punishments were to be handed out to anyone who dared step out of line.

And the rogues had been aplenty. Whit often welcomed them into his office, and there were often no fewer than six or seven sailors a day; many of whom were experiencing high levels of stress and strain brought on by the Captain's new restrictions. And more than a few of them were facing Captain's Mast for having violated said restrictions.

One poor soul had committed the "inexcusable and selfish act" (Worst-gen's words) of visiting his mother at an off-base restaurant. Another person had been caught attending church. Both were now suspended from training on how to operate nuclear reactors, and were now emptying garbage cans on base.

For most of his young adult life, Whit had idealized

the military. There was simply no pedestal too high for the calling that he was sure had been his, and his indefinitely. When 9/11 happened, Whit had leapt onto the George W. Bush-led bandwagon of ridding the world of global Islamic terror. Such a worldwide scourge simply had to be stopped, and the U.S. military – in all of its red, white, and blue glory – was just the instrument that Almighty God was going to use to stop it.

Looking back, he had been a damned fool for even entertaining the thought.

As his status as a Navy chaplain had evolved, so had his ideology, and the more his eyes opened, the more aware he became that "Freedom", once an anthem to live by, was now little more than a punchline. The politicians – who directly controlled the livelihood to which Whit had pledged himself and upon which he had pinned his family's hopes and dreams – lied continually; and never more so than when they used words like "opportunity" and "heritage" and (on increasingly fewer occasions, Whit noted) "liberty".

He loved his fellow sailors, loved counseling them and helping them through life's troubles and tribulations; but that's about where it ended. Other than that, he hated the Navy, and wanted out – promotion to the next pay grade be damned.

Whit explained – or tried to explain – all of this to Dr. Allenby. The truth was that he hated talking about himself, especially when it came to discussing his life's struggles with perfect strangers.

As a chaplain, he had no problem listening. And yet, he figured he was like most caregivers; able to give, but not receive, when it came to the vital care and relief that most people needed. Maybe part of it, he mused at times, was the burden that it often accompanied; a burden he knew all too well - the emotional and spiritual toll that came with providing care. Why inflict it on someone else and force them to carry it for you?

The logic was almost perverse, but it was ever-present just the same.

Still, as he tried to explain himself to Dr. Allenby, he found himself rambling at times, stumbling at other times, and overall just failing to find the right words more than he succeeded at it.

Dr. Allenby just sat and nodded affirmingly, gently prodding him with the same nonverbal gesticulations that Whit often used when he was the one counseling.

When Whit had finished, Dr. Allenby sat motionless for a moment, as if he was processing everything Whit had told him. Finally, he looked up and stated, "Thank you, Whit…for sharing that with me."

Whit managed a faint nod.

"Tell me about these thoughts you've had," Dr. Allenby continued, keeping his kindly gaze on him.

Whit studied him for a moment. "About giving up?"

Dr. Allenby nodded.

Whit shifted in his seat, and tried to meet the doctor's gaze. Maybe it was shame, or perhaps vulnerability, but looking into the knowing eyes of Dr. Cloyce Allenby at that moment was next to impossible for some reason.

"Are you afraid?" Dr. Allenby asked.

"Afraid of what?"

Dr. Allenby shrugged. "I don't know," he clarified. "Fear is an emotion; a perfectly legitimate one; and one we all experience. Question is, do you feel it? Only if you answer yes can we begin to unpack why it is you might feel that way."

It made sense, and Whit almost hated the doctor for it. This was his lane – counseling and talking to people about their emotional and spiritual issues - and yet here he was, feeling as though he was unable to grasp such a basic dynamic of the human psyche, right here in the doctor's office.

Whit suddenly felt small and wanted to get the hell out of there.

"It's okay, Whit," Dr. Allenby said, as if he was reading Whit's troubled mind once again. "You don't have to have all the answers here. In fact, getting help requires that you take off your caregiver hat, and let someone else wear theirs."

Strangely, this had a calming effect, and Whit felt his spine relax. For the first time, he realized that it had stiffened and was causing him to sit up in an uncomfortable posture for God only knew how long.

"So again," Dr. Allenby persisted, "what are you afraid of?"

Whit thought for another moment. He thought of his job, the failure to select for promotion, the constant feelings of inadequacy that came with his job; his disillusionment; his command's ill treatment of its members; all of it… every one of his woes were thrust through his cortex in an effort to pinpoint the answer to the doctor's question.

"I guess…" he began, his eyes darting around the room. "…I guess I'm just tired."

Dr. Allenby nodded, barely budging. "Go on," he urged. "What are you tired of?"

Whit was good with words, but he was now struggling to come up with just the right ones. And yet, in the midst of the uncertainty, he felt he was coming to a realization.

Images flashed through his mind, as the crystallization of what he felt he was truly "tired" of came closer to the surface; images of his previous command down in Florida; where he had first learned of his failure to select for promotion the first time around.

There were images of his current command; pictures that Whit knew would be indelibly etched into his mind forever; those of Worst-gen sneering and promising to re-strict the freedoms of the people under his command – laughing off with nary a shrug the complaints of those who pushed back on the COVID restrictions. *Fuck them,* Whit had heard him say in reference to the students at NNPTS who had mustered the courage to ask honest questions of their captain about his intentions regarding how to mitigate COVID. Many of these same students had found their way to Whit's office and sobbed when told of their inability to see family for the foreseeable fu-ture due to being locked down at base. Whit had done his best with what little he had to console them.

*Fuck them,* was Worst-gen's response.

And Whit could do nothing about it; the same way he could do nothing about the Navy's position on his perfor-mance as a chaplain (*Fuck you, Lieutenant Whit Gregg… you are not selected for promotion*).

The answer was now almost as clear as day.

As Whit's emotions came to the surface once more, so did a solitary word that Whit had had his finger on for some time now, but only now was able to finally vocalize and give voice to. It was a word he hated; a word that was antithetical to everything he felt human beings ought to stand for and aspire to in their short lives; a word that stood in direct adversity and opposition to the very dig-nity and inherent potency that he felt human beings were afforded in their status as created beings of an Almighty God.

It was a word he hated with every fiber of his being.

*Powerless.*

He hated that God-forsaken word.

"I'm tired…" Whit almost whispered, unable to look Dr. Allenby in the eyes, "…of feeling powerless."

# Chapter 7

Whit didn't know what to expect from Dr. Allenby when he'd said the word.

*Powerless...*

It had so many connotations in the world that Whit lived in. On one hand, Whit's own religious faith taught that "powerlessness" was the way to go when it came to intimacy with God. *Only after you have truly realized your own inability to do anything can God truly begin to work in and through your life. Only then can you really be used as an instrument by Him.*

It sounded great, and Whit wanted to believe it...did believe it, in fact. But, as with everything else, there was a cost. And the cost of powerlessness was pressure...and pain.

Pressure and pain; two concepts that Whit felt deeply; two themes that resulted from his own inherent, primal need to have some say-so - however small - over his own destiny and life. The pressure and pain he felt resulted from his own self-determination being snatched away from him on a whim; taken in stride by men and women with no remorse and no regard for human life and dignity.

Christianity called it "pride"…"sinful pride", at that. But Whit wasn't so sure anymore. The acuteness of what he felt as a result of the actions of the powerful people in his world had him questioning many aspects of his life, and particularly in regard to his faith. Perhaps the tenuous relationship between "humility" and "human dignity" was one of those areas.

Dr. Allenby's tender eyes never blinked, and he nodded as if he not only understood, but had also perhaps once been there himself not too long ago.

"It definitely sucks to feel powerless," he said in a ginger tone.

"It sucks, but…" Whit began.

"But what?"

"I guess in some ways, feeling powerless is a good thing because it reminds you of who you really are. Maybe we all need reminders of the fact that we really are powerless when you get right down to it."

Now, Dr. Allenby seemed to suppress a grin, and maybe even a chuckle. "That's true," he affirmed. "We can learn a lot from having power taken from us; Jesus knew about that all too well. We grow closer to Him when we share in his sufferings."

He paused.

"However," Dr. Allenby continued, "I've often wondered just how damaging to our souls it can be to have one of the most fundamental impulses suppressed, if not completely taken from us."

Whit studied him.

"I'm speaking of self-determination," Dr. Allenby said. "As Christians, we live under the headship of the Holy Spirit. But we also are granted free will. Of course, the struggle to understand free will versus God's sovereignty is a conversation that is as old as theology itself. But we still ought to never minimize the role of free will and self-government when trying to understand the human condition."

Whit was listening with rapt attention.

"I suppose what I am saying is that your feelings are valid, Whit," he affirmed.

Dr. Allenby's fatherly gaze melted Whit's heart, and he felt emotion that he had forgotten that he had welling up within him. Using the back of his hand, he wiped away tears.

Dr. Allenby handed him a box of tissues. Whit took one as he listened to him continue.

"The impulse we have for freedom of life, movement, and determining our own choices is a strong one," he said. "So strong is it, in fact, that to suppress it in any way, whether we ourselves are doing the suppressing or someone else is doing it, at the end of the day it really is almost an affront to our identity as created beings."

"Yeah," Whit said, crumpling the tissue in his hand.

"Powerlessness is a terrible thing," Dr. Allenby said. "And that is why your feelings are valid."

Whit now felt lighter than he had upon entering Dr. Allenby's office. Somehow, he had been expecting an upbraiding of some kind for how he had been feeling, only to now instead feel understood and seen. It felt liberating in a way that Whit had not felt in a long time.

"Thankfully," Dr. Allenby went on, "powerlessness is like most other unpleasant places in which we often find ourselves, in that we don't have to stay there."

"What do you mean?" Whit asked.

"What I mean is simply that there are ways in which you can leave the powerlessness behind you."

"How do I do that?"

Dr. Allenby took a sip of water from a nearby bottle and grinned as he gave a faint nod of the head. "First, ask yourself this: what is the opposite of powerlessness?"

"Power."

"That's right," Dr. Allenby affirmed. "In your case, that means finding a place of power. More to the point, it involves learning to identify a place of power…within you."

Whit sensed that old familiar weight coming back upon him once more. The light airiness which he had felt only moments before was now gone, and his mind now sought to process just how he might find a "place of pow-er", as Dr. Allenby was describing it.

"You don't know how to do that, do you?" Dr. Allenby said, ever the mind-reader.

Whit shook his head, and felt ashamed once more.

"It's difficult," Dr. Allenby said, "to think of a place where you feel, or have felt, powerful, when all you feel in the present is a lack of power."

Whit nodded in agreement.

"But that's why I'm not asking you to think of the present," he continued. "Rather, I'm inviting you to think of a time when the only thing you did feel was power. Can you think of a time in your life that's like that?"

Moments later, Whit sat with a pen and notepad on his lap…thinking.

Dr. Allenby sat waiting…quietly and patiently.

Whit racked his brain, trying to come up with a mem-ory – or inkling of a memory – in which he felt "power-ful", whatever that even meant.

And that was the rub; what did it mean? There was the Power Of God, that much was true; something Whit for certain believed in. But it was usually characterized in terms of mere mortals being power*less*, and…well…what was the point of dwelling on that? Why think about that when you felt as though your own power had been eviscerated?

His mind was racing, but seemed at the same time somehow tethered to Dr. Allenby's wise words.

*The impulse we have for freedom of life, movement, and determining our own choices is a strong one…so strong is it, in fact, that to suppress it in any way, whether we ourselves are doing the suppressing or someone else is doing it, at the end of the day it really is an affront to our identity as created beings.*

Even in his mind's hot, troubled state, Whit found himself marveling at the ease with which he could remember what Dr. Allenby had said with such eloquence.

And so, he struggled; grappling against the element of human nature that causes mankind to forget their most treasured memories. And as he struggled, he was certain that if there ever had been a time in his life when he had felt "powerful", that surely that moment in his existence would spring to the forefront of his conscience at a time like this.

Unless of course there had never been such a time in his life. In that case, he figured the only way forward was consignment to whatever despair awaited him. Because the truth was that very little of his own life had felt like a case study in power and strength, and more like a study of cowardice and the angst that results. Too often, Whit had been content to let folks get the better of him; whether in grade school, middle school, high school, or adult-hood. Kids were mean; adults were, too. But wasn't it the purview of individuals to stand up for themselves? Why couldn't he, then? Why had he not?

The stream of thought made him anxious, and he began to doodle on the paper. Using the horizontal, ruled lines of the notebook page, Whit began to complement them with vertical lines, thereby creating individual squares on the paper. The pen was a black-ink instrument and, strangely enough, caused Whit to subliminally long for color. It was not an intense yearning; not the kind you experience when missing a loved one; but a desire just the same. In that moment, he found himself wanting to create art; even if it was with a box of crayons, like he'd had in kindergarten.

*Art…color…crayons…kindergarten…*

Something in his memory bank was stirring.

He was back in kindergarten; Mrs. Barrett's class. There were crayons, set in the center of a round table, and Whit was seated on one side of it. Next to him was a girl… a female classmate of his…what was her name? Courtney? Kayla?

She was crying.

Her clothes were dirty; not filthy and tattered, but dirty, just the same. Unkempt, as if only minimal care had been given to her as she had prepared to go to school that morning.

In his mind's eye, Whit saw this dejected girl reach for the box of crayons, only to have her hand swatted away by…someone; who? A nameless face?

It was coming clearer now; the slapper-away-of-hands, the tormentor. The sneering girl guarding the crayons had blonde hair and a petulant look that bespoke her officious and self-serving nature. Whit hated her immediately, even if his mind was lax in recalling exactly who she was. (*Karen, Kara, Karla…*)

Karman.

Yes, of course! Karman. The Teacher's Pet in his kindergarten class. And also The Enforcer when it came to Mrs. Barrett's rules in the classroom; and no rule was too arbitrary to be enforced, when Karman had her way.

It was all coming back now.

What was her last name? Whit decided to not push it. His memory was in overdrive as it was.

In fact, he was doing well to remember the episode at the table with the crayons now; all of which was beginning to come into focus like a film reel through a camera lens. Whit now saw the yellow table in full view, saw the assortment of dirty crayons in a square box, creating something akin to a drab rainbow, saw Courtney (if that was her name) with the dirty clothes sitting next to him, despondent over her rejected efforts to get a crayon and – perhaps – create some kind of beauty in her otherwise dreary life.

He also saw Karman The Enforcer reaching across the table and swatting little Courtney's hand away.

*No! Mrs. Barrett said not to use the crayons yet!* (Whit remembered that now. He also remembered thinking that Mrs. Barrett had said no such thing, and that Karman – per usual – was simply letting herself get carried away with the power given to her).

As Whit reflected, he found himself getting angry… again. Injustice was everywhere, had always been everywhere, and was often at its most poignant and memorable during the tenderest years of one's life. Jesus, was it really possible to hate a kindergarten child when you were almost forty? He almost had to laugh. How many years had it been since he had seen Karman in Mrs. Barrett's class? And yet, he still found himself getting pissed at how she had swatted a classmate's hand away for just wanting to create something; all based on a lie about what the teacher had really said.

Another memory surfaced; this one strangely assuaging his angst somehow. In his mind's eye, Whit saw himself standing up from his chair beside Courtney, a look of righteous indignation in his eyes – though he himself could not see it. Karman could see it. Whit saw her stand up – as if to swat *his* hand away. And yet, as she took notice of his angry demeanor, she sat back down as quickly as she had stood. Whit had stared her down; stared down the bully.

Whit watched as his kindergarten self reached into the crayon box, took out a handful of assorted crayons, and gave them to Courtney. Within moments, her crying had subsided, and her tear-stained face was focused on what appeared to be a barnyard and horse pasture which she drew and colored on her paper. She gave Whit only passing attention, but also gave him a faint smile when she shook her head in response to his asking if she needed any additional crayons.

Karmen did not bother either of them for the rest of the day.

Whit looked at the page in astonishment. Over the past fifteen minutes, he had been somewhat conscious of the fact that he had been writing. And yet, that silly Kindergarten memory had, in a strange way, consumed him…not to mention, validated him somehow. Maybe his life had been something other than a case study of powerlessness after all.

"Can I see?" Dr. Allenby broke the silence, reaching his hand forward in a kindly manner.

Whit handed him the paper and sat back, still in awe of the fact that he had been writing while wholly consumed by the recollection.

Dr. Allenby, for his part, focused his eyes on the paper, and was smiling.

Whit hoped this was a good thing.

"Stood up to the bully, did you?" Dr. Allenby asked with a smile, after he had finished reading. "That's power-ful."

Whit shrugged. "More or less."

"A lot of people would say 'more'", Dr. Allenby re-joined. "What happened to Courtney? Any idea?"

Whit shook his head. "I don't remember," he an-swered. "I don't think she was at our school the next year."

"Think she would remember you?"

Whit thought for a moment "Maybe."

Dr. Allenby shifted in his seat. "Do you think you'd remember someone who did for you what you did for her? Even if it was a small thing?" he asked Whit.

"Maybe."

"You remembered what happened so many years ago, so how likely is it that she would too?"

Dr. Allenby had a point.

"Are there any other stories or examples of you helping someone? Or helping to maybe *empower* someone? Like you did with," he checked the paper again, "Courtney."

Whit was silent again as he pondered the question. Glancing through a window, he had a partial view of the street traffic just outside of Dr. Allenby's office. A bus ambled by, making a dull roar as it passed, and Whit's memory began to foment once again.

He turned back to Dr. Allenby.

"Your face definitely seems to be saying 'yes'", he beamed at Whit.

"When I was in seminary," Whit began, "sometimes I would have to ride the bus to work. It was back in 2007. Gas prices were pretty high then, so I didn't have a lot to spend on fuel. Driving only happened when I needed it to."

Dr. Allenby nodded.

"There was one weekend in particular," he continued, "where I got on the bus near campus, and was headed in the direction of the restaurant where I worked. I guess one neat thing about public transportation is that you get so that you can 'recognize the regulars', as we always said at the restaurant. Public transportation and food service; that's one thing they have in common. You get to know people, and get used to seeing them – whether they come into your place of work, or get on the bus with you.

"Anyway, this one day, I get on the bus, and a few stops later, a girl gets on that I'd never seen before." He paused and grinned. "I knew I'd never seen her before, because I would have for sure recognized her otherwise. She looked like she'd gone months without going near a washing machine or a shower. Smelled like it, too. She was about thirteen or fourteen, I'd say; just a kid, and the streets had already pretty much spit her out, from the way she looked."

Whit paused, unsure if he wanted to go into what happened next.

"That wasn't the worst of it, though. Next thing I notice is the plastic bag in her hand. She kind of had it concealed under her sweatshirt sleeve, which was kind of loose on her."

Whit stopped again, and glanced out the window, this time wishing that a bus would come and pick him up somehow so that he didn't have to do this. *Magic Bus… wasn't that a famous '60s song, or something?*

"Go on," Dr. Allenby urged.

Whit took a deep breath. "Every few seconds, she'd raise that plastic bag to her nose and inhale; then she'd put it back down."

Dr. Allenby studied him.

"Glue," Whit said. "I didn't smell it for several minutes, but when I got a whiff of it, I finally understood what she was doing. So did everyone else on that bus."

"What happened then?"

Whit shook his head. "People got pissed. I mean, here we are, all living the minimum wage life – and below – and these folks are acting like they're better than this poor girl just trying to make it through another day; and using a glue fix to make it happen."

Dr. Allenby nodded.

"And there was one guy in particular," Whit continued, "about in his mid-thirties. Soon as he smelled the glue, he jumps up and just goes ballistic on this girl; gets in her face, screams at her for bringing a 'toxic-smelling substance' into an enclosed area like this; accuses her of trying to get people high; tells her she's a waste of space…"

Whit paused, as emotion began roiling up inside him. He put his head in his hands, and tried to fight back tears. Dr. Allenby gave him space.

"Then," Whit continued, "he pushed her head against the window where she was sitting."

Dr. Allenby seemed to wince, but kept his sympathetic eyes on Whit. "What about the bus driver, Whit? What did he do?"

*"Fuck all,"* Whit barely whispered, regretting it right away.

"What was that?" Dr. Allenby asked.

"I shouldn't have said that," Whit answered ruefully. "What I should have said is that he didn't do anything."

Dr. Allenby nodded, seemingly unbothered by Whit's knee-jerk use of profanity. "So the bus driver did nothing."

Whit shook his head.

"But what did you do?"

Whit thought for a moment, before gathering himself. "When he pushed her head against the window, I jumped up and got between them. I just couldn't take it anymore.

And I told him that if he laid another hand on that girl, that I'd personally throw his fat ass off of that bus."

Dr. Allenby was a counselor, as was Whit; so they both knew about the need to keep one's emotions – or at least one's emotional reactions and facial expressions – in check during a session. Still, Whit could not help but notice what appeared to be a look of grim, sadistic glee on the face of Cloyce Allenby as he told the story.

"And then what happened?" Dr. Allenby asked.

"He backed down," Whit answered. "Sat back in his seat. I guess most cowards would have done the same thing."

"I'd say so," Dr. Allenby agreed. "And what about the girl?"

Whit smiled. "Turns out, we got off the bus at the same stop. The place I worked at was a small, deli-style outfit that made good sandwiches. So I had her wait outside, and then I had one of our cooks make her a hoagie after I clocked in."

"Did you ever see her again?"

Whit shook his head. The truth was, in the thirteen years since it had happened, Whit had nearly forgotten about the entire episode. This frustrated him.

*Why in the hell is it so difficult to remember the moments of our lives when we're our best selves, but our lousiest moments play like a damn movie reel in our heads?*

"You seem like you had to work a little bit to recall

that memory," Dr. Allenby commented, seeing into his head once more.

"Yeah," Whit admitted. "Unfortunately."

"That is unfortunate," Dr. Allenby said, "because that definitely sounds like a Davidity moment, if you ask me."

Whit studied him. "A what?"

Dr. Allenby grinned. "A little word I made up."

"Divinity?" Whit asked.

"DAVIDity," Dr. Allenby corrected, emphasizing the first two syllables. "From King David, who wasn't always a king."

Whit nodded.

"I'm assuming you know the story," Dr. Allenby said to him. "About David…the shepherd-boy-turned-king."

Whit nodded. Of course he did.

"When he fought Goliath, David had to reach much deeper within himself for what mattered most than he ever did for a giant-killing stone," Dr. Allenby went on. "When Goliath presented himself, that was David's moment. He had the chance to step up and do what he knew needed to be done; to protect his people, and himself. Thankfully, that was a chance he took, but only after finding it within himself to do so. And it paid off. And the rest, as they say, is history."

"Davidity," Whit said, almost to himself.

"The truth is, Whit," Dr. Allenby continued, "you've got a lot more going for you than your feelings of being pushed around, and feeling powerless. I listen to you, and you're the guy helping those who can't help themselves. That's power. And that's Davidity."

"Yeah," Whit agreed. "I just wish I could translate that power into helping…"

"…helping those in your care?" Dr. Allenby asked.

Whit nodded.

"Those having their lives and freedoms and dignity trampled upon?"

"Yeah," Whit said. "I don't know how any of what I've told you translates into how to help them."

Dr. Allenby thought for a moment. "Maybe it's not for you to know yet."

Whit considered this for a moment, then nodded.

"Of course, that's one area that prayer can help you in," Dr. Allenby continued. "You can always pray for opportunities to step up and help those who don't have a voice." He grinned. "It sure seems to have helped you in your younger days; both in kindergarten and on that bus."

Whit thought about it. He thought about his life which, he now thought, was probably more akin to the lives of many people; not marked by a single point of failure, or even multiple points of failure. Hell, it wasn't even marked by single or numerous points of success. Like most things, it was diverse…messy, even; the victories and defeats as numerous each as the grains of sand on a seashore. All of it was intermixed and intertwined, making a beautiful amalgamation of a life lived, and – just perhaps – a life lived well.

Whit smiled at Dr. Allenby and gave him a faint nod. "Maybe so, Doctor," he agreed. "Maybe so."

# CHAPTER 8

In theory, Commander's Morning Muster was an opportunity for the Site staff to assemble in the commander's conference room on the third floor each morning. Its purpose, at least on paper, was to ensure that everyone was aligned with the current plan of the day.

In practice, however, it was really just an opportunity for Captain Andrew Bestgen to hear the sound of his own voice, and ensure that everyone within earshot heard it too.

Whit's Captain loved to hear himself talk. And staff members, including Whit, were required to listen to it each morning.

Everyone stood in a circle around the large conference table in the command suite and went round-robin-style, each person briefing the captain about whatever they had on the agenda for the day, or whatever was coming up.

When each staff member had spoken, it was Worstgen's turn. He took over the floor and usually did not relinquish it for the next fifteen to twenty minutes, during which he blustered on and on about whatever was on his mind that morning, and after which he dismissed everyone and sent them on their separate ways.

Whit estimated that between seventy-five and ninety percent of what came out of Worst-gen's mouth during this daily stretch could easily be shared via email, phone calls, and private conversations with the people who most needed to hear it – which usually did not include Whit.

For his own part, Whit seldom shared anything when his turn came around, and usually replied with a simple "nothing for the group, sir." There were two reasons for this: one, because he often truly did not have anything to share. And two, because he knew that the less was said by himself and everyone else, the sooner they could all leave after Worst-gen's latest soliloquy. It sometimes made him grin when he realized that fewer and fewer people were saying anything anymore when their turns came around during the meetings. He did not know for certain, but he suspected that wanting to get the hell out of the conference room was a big part of the reason why.

Whatever the case was, Whit soon found himself of the third floor and dreading the next fifteen minutes.

He checked his watch; *ten minutes early, good time,* and – almost reflexively – felt himself starting to get pissed. Senior officers, as a whole, were notorious for making junior officers wait for them to start meetings, and Worst-gen often distinguished himself from this group by not only wandering in late to his own meetings, but also by seeming to *relish* doing so.

Sure enough, he was late again this morning – eight minutes this time – and sure enough, JAG was with him when he entered the conference room.

Lieutenant Jade Kulkarni, of the Judge Advocate General (JAG) Corps of the Navy, served as Worst-gen's legal adviser and closest confidante at the command. She tottered in behind him like a geisha girl and, despite the mask she wore, sported a bright smile that Whit had no problem discerning was there.

She was about thirty years old, attractive and blonde, and her blue eyes and easy smile often made for good first impressions. In addition to that, her curves in all the right places often made for easy flirtation when she interacted with the senior leadership of the command during Morning Muster.

Whit knew, however, that what really endeared her to the hearts of the Site senior leadership was her ability to "break sailors".

"I didn't mean to make him cry," JAG said to Worst-gen in a playful tone, as the two of them entered.

Her eyes, the only facial feature not concealed by a mask, sparkled as if she were mock-pleading with him for mercy and understanding.

"Yeah, I'm calling bull shit," Worst-gen responded,

glancing at her with a jovial expression that – even with his own mask – was easy to read.

Captain Andrew Bestgen was a tallish man of about fifty; with graying hair, and a fluid walk that, if not for his rank and position, would seem almost listless. As it was, he carried himself as someone who had authority, and knew it, and was therefore in no hurry to move quickly on behalf of anyone but himself.

"Call bull shit all you want," JAG rejoined. "I'm a nice person."

This drew laughter from the other people in the room; mostly male senior enlisted leaders and officers of various stripes, who cast lustful and appreciative looks in her direction.

"Nice people don't promote in the Navy, JAG," Worstgen rejoined. "And at the rate you're going, you'll get a meritorious promotion for all the sailors you've torn to shreds."

JAG's eyes sparkled with ambition, as the room erupted in laughter and affirmation of what the Captain had just said.

"JAG's mean."

"You don't go into JAG's office and leave without a Kleenex in hand."

"JAG eats sailors' souls for breakfast."

"I am not mean!" JAG protested, keeping up the flirtatious play as everyone took their positions around the conference table.

It was all true, though, and no one knew it better than Whit. *Piece of shit…garbage human being…disgrace to your family…* those were just a few of the *tame* monikers that JAG had assigned to sailors who had run afoul the Captain's COVID rules since the restrictions had been in place. Whit knew this because of the myriad of them who had come to his office after a "JAG run-in".

He despised her almost as much as he disdained Worst-gen.

It was one thing to hold a sailor accountable for wrongdoing, but it was another thing to *revel with glee* the way JAG (and others) were doing now because of the way they inflicted emotional pain on the 18- and 19-year old sailors who were away from home for the first time.

It was beyond reprehensible.

"So who's wiping away tears today, JAG?" asked one hefty chief, whose eyes, Whit noticed, discreetly fluttered between JAG's face and her tits.

"Hartman," JAG answered, almost as an afterthought, glancing at her notebook and becoming immersed in something else. "Seaman Rose Hartman."

"What'd she do again?" Worst-gen asked, taking his designated spot at the head of the conference table, and seeming to forget the indefensible thing he'd said to Rose Hartman just days earlier.

"Went to a beach house with her boyfriend; got caught."

"Oh yeah," Worst-gen said, laughing. "Tried to get my sailors sick by running wild during COVID. Shitbag."

Whit's blood boiled.

The men in the room laughed, including the captain.

"So on that note," Worst-gen stated, "that's a pretty good segue right into this morning's agenda. We'll obviously be going over the case of Seaman Hartman…the little fucker who decided it would be okay to go out during a pandemic and get laid or something."

"Can't wait!" JAG exclaimed, as if looking forward to a hot date on Friday.

Whit tuned out the rest of the meeting, and prayed that time would somehow hurry up so that he could leave…the conference room, as well as – later on – the Navy itself.

Fifteen minutes later, he was still in the conference room, still surrounded by many of the same people who had attended Morning Muster.

Worst-gen and JAG had stepped out to go over some last-minute details regarding the case of Seaman Rose Hartman, and her impending Captain's Mast.

Whit just sat in a leather-bound chair next to the wall and waited.

Worst-gen soon reappeared and took his seat at the head of the long conference table. Within moments, Seaman Rose Hartman would stand on the opposite end of it, facing the commanding officer, who had earlier spent about ten minutes denigrating her name in a room full of officers and senior enlisted.

Whit shook his head, and prayed that it would be over soon.

"We ready?" Worst-gen said to JAG, who nodded. "Bring her in," he instructed the Master-At-Arms.

One by one, the officers in the room, including Whit, rose and stood upright at the position of attention; erect posture, shoulders back, and hands smartly planted at the sides of their thighs.

The Master-At-Arms was a short, plump sailor, who wore a yellow badge sewn to his uniform blouse, and – at the captain's signal - opened the conference room door. He then positioned himself next to the doorway, and turned, facing the far wall of the conference room as he himself stood at the position of attention.

"ACCUSED…ENTER!" he bellowed.

There was a long pause, as Seaman Rose Hartman marched her way from the hallway leading into the conference room, through the door, and toward the far end of the conference room table, where she stood opposite Captain Andrew Bestgen, but did not face him.

The Master-At-Arms followed her, as was his duty, and proceeded to give her instructions as she took her place in the room.

"Left face!" he ordered in a sharp, official tone.

Rose did as she was told and faced the Captain's direction.

"Hand salute!"

On cue, Rose's stiffened right hand went to her right eyebrow in a crisp, perfect salute.

"Report!"

"Good morning, sir. Seaman Hartman reporting to Captain's Mast as ordered, sir," Hartman stated.

"Very well," Worst-gen returned.

"Two!" ordered the Master-At-Arms.

Rose dropped her right hand back to her side at the position of attention.

"Uncover!"

Rose's right hand snapped back to the top tip of the garrison cover which she wore on her head, which she pinched with her index finger and thumb.

"Two!"

At the command of the Master-At-Arms, she quickly doffed her cover.

"Seaman Hartman," Worst-gen began, "you are suspected of committing the following violation of the Uniform Code of Military Justice: Article ninety-two, in that you willfully disobeyed a lawful order by going to a beach house, which was a violation of my rules issued as an effort to mitigate the spread of COVID-19. You do not have to make any statement regarding the offense of which you have been accused, and any statement made by you can be used as evidence against you.

"You are advised that a non-judicial punishment is not a trial, and that a determination of misconduct on your part is not a conviction by a court. You are further advised that the formal rules of evidence used in trials by courts-martial do not apply at nonjudicial punishment.

"I have a statement signed by you acknowledging that you were fully advised of your legal rights pertaining at this hearing. Do you understand this statement and do you understand the rights explained therein?

"Yes sir," Rose answered in a meek tone.

"Do you have any questions concerning your rights?" Worst-gen continued.

"No sir."

I also have before me the evidence binder in your case. Have you been given a chance to examine it?

"Yes sir."

Worst-gen paused, and seemed to be collecting his thoughts, almost as if he were unsure as to how he would now address the sailor. But Whit knew better. He had sat through enough Captain's Masts to know that once the scripted legal formalities were out of the way, Worst-gen had every intention of giving the accused, helpless sailor a full and complete excoriation.

He hated this next part.

"Why'd you do it?" Worst-gen asked simply, training his eyes upon Rose Hartman. Even with the mask that covered his nose and mouth, Whit could discern the look of haughtiness and disdain with which his commanding officer regarded the young sailor. Worst-gen's eyes told the story.

*Eyes are the windows to the soul.*

Every part of Rose Hartman looked as though it was paralyzed by fear at that moment. She remained upright at the position of attention, but her body seemed to make a slight, involuntary rocking motion as she fought to stammer out her version of the right response.

Meanwhile, every other member of her chain of command who was in attendance seemed to cast jeering stares at her as she struggled.

Whit loathed them all at that moment.

"I…" she began.

"Answer the Captain!" the heavyset Master-At-Arms instructed in a tone of voice that was both gentle and angry.

"I…I just wanted to see my boyfriend."

"Mmmhmm," Worst-gen mocked. "You wanted to see your boyfriend."

Moments passed, as Worst-gen pretended to consider Rose's response.

"I understand," Worst-gen finally broke the silence. "It's a rough time, and yeah…we all have folks that we want to see; boyfriends, girlfriends, family, close friends, you name it."

He paused and took a deep breath.

"The problem, of course, is that we're in the middle of a fucking pandemic, Seaman Hartman."

Worst-gen's tone of voice, and the anger therein, was rising with each syllable.

"So yeah, while I can be sympathetic to your wanting to get away and see your boyfriend, or close friends, or whoever, the reality is that I can't take on the added responsibility of letting you go and fulfill whatever childish desire comes to your mind right away. Do you understand what I'm telling you?"

"Yes sir."

"You broke my COVID rules, which means that you not only willfully and unduly put yourself in harm's way, but you…" Worst-gen paused again, his reddening face bearing out that he was fighting to control the rage he felt at this nineteen-year-old sailor. "…you also put my sailors in harm's way also."

Whit glanced over at Rose, whose composure was waning in tandem with Worst-gen's ability to hold back his wrath. Tears were forming in her eyes, and Whit saw the same familiar red splotches that he had seen days earlier during their last counseling session.

"You're crying now," Worst-gen observed. "I guess that's understandable, too. You know who else I've seen cry before?"

A pause.

"I asked you a question," Worst-gen persisted.

The Master-At-Arms stepped forward so that his face was just inches from Rose's. "You will answer your commanding officer!" he ordered loudly.

"No sir," Rose barely squeaked.

"The same pieces of shit I masted for sexual harassment not too long ago," Worst-gen sneered from behind his mask. "Yeah, that's right. Those bastards shed a few tears in the place you're standing right now, too; after they were the ones caught making unwanted advances on their fellow sailors – MY sailors. They cried like small children, the same way you're doing now."

Whit now saw Rose's chest heaving as uncontrollable sobs racked her body.

"So forgive me, Seaman Hartman, if I fail to show any sympathy for you, because to my mind – and I've said this before – you're no better in my sight than those bastards are. Sexual harasser, sexual predator, COVID rules violator; all of you put my sailors in danger. And all of you deserve to be punished. You're no different; remember that."

Rose's knees seemed to be weakening as her body fell under the invisible weight of Worst-gen's condemnation of her. A few of the officers were grinning from behind their masks. Whit glanced over at JAG who seemed to beam at the scene unfolding before her.

Whit tried to somehow dislocate or disassociate himself from what was happening before him. But it was to no avail.

"For the chain of command," Worst-gen continued, turning his attention away from the shattered sailor in front of him to the wall of officers and leaders that were assembled on his left flank, "what can you tell me about Seaman Hartman's performance of duty?"

Now it was their turn. Rose's leading petty officer, her class director, her class officer, the senior enlisted leader at the "A" school, the "A" school director, the command master chief, and the executive officer – all of them chimed in. While a few of them made an overture at Rose's otherwise solid performance record, most of them zeroed in on her misconduct. A couple of them even agreed with the Captain's assessment of her; specifically the comparison to a sexual predator.

When they had finished, Worst-gen turned back to Rose. "You've heard the chain of command. Is there anything else that you would like to say in response?"

A long pause, as Rose – still sobbing – tried to crawl out from under the weight of the accusations heaped upon her by men and women that she would likely never outrank during her military service.

"No sir."

"Are you sure?" Worst-gen pressed, almost teasing her. "This is your chance to say something for yourself."

"I…" Rose managed to almost whisper, her voice still choked by incessant sobs. "I…just…want to say I'm sorry."

Worst-gen's eyebrows arched, as if he were somehow surprised by her tacit admission of guilt.

"Yeah," he half-affirmed. "I can see that. Most folks

get to that point when they're caught, and they know they're about to be held accountable. It's human nature, I guess. Of course, it in no way changes the reality of the matter; which is that you're just as big a piece of garbage as that sexual predator I masted a while back. But yeah, the repentance part is understandable, though."

Worst-gen paused and gestured toward Whit. "Chaps, here, can help you with that later, I guess," he said. "But as for me, my give-a-fuck is pretty much busted."

Everyone in the room, with the exception of a seething Chaplain Whit Gregg, was laughing. JAG, in particular, was giggling like a school girl.

Whit's hands balled into fists, and he tried to push from his psyche the urge to grab the thick, solid chair behind him and hurl it at his commanding officer; at the jeering, sniveling, teenage bully of a man who outranked him, and knew it. At that moment, Whit's frail human nature wanted nothing more than to see Andrew Bestgen's skull crushed by whichever part of that chair hit him between the eyes – like David's stone hit Goliath.

*Jesus,* Whit prayed harder than he had in a while.

When the laughter had died down, Worst-gen went on as he glanced at Rose's file folder.

"Are you sure there is nothing else that you would like to present here today?"

"No sir," Rose squeaked. "I've already made my statement."

At this, Worst-gen looked up. "Already made your statement?"

"Yes, sir," Rose answered. "It's in my folder."

Worst-gen's brow furrowed, as he returned to fumbling through the orange folder once more, not stopping until he came to a particular document that seemed to hold his interest. Whit watched as his Captain's facial features relaxed while he read the document, though he also noted that they did not relax in a way that necessarily conveyed relief.

After a few moments of reading, Worst-gen sat almost upright, and turned to where Rose's chain of command remained standing at attention.

"Petty Officer Duff," Worst-gen addressed a short, pudgy sailor whom Whit recognized as Rose's immediate class supervisor. "This statement…"

"Yes, sir," Duff said, stepping forward. A look of uneasiness was in his eyes. "We were conducting the initial interview shortly after calling Seaman Hartman into the office, and we took down her statement during the course of that."

"Did she agree to giving the statement prior to your asking for it?" Worst-gen demanded of Duff.

"Sir, she…"

"Let me back up," Worst-gen waved him off, "Was she informed that she did not have to make a statement, prior to her making this statement?"

Duff became helpless, as his widened eyes glanced to his left – to *his* immediate supervisor – who gave him a sidelong glance that was non-committal.

Whit was no legal expert, but he sensed in that moment that a legal blunder of some kind had been committed.

There was an uncomfortable silence, which Worst-gen broke after only a few seconds.

"I'd like for Seaman Hartman to leave the room," Worst-gen almost barked to the Master-At-Arms.

"Cover!" the Master-At-Arms barked at Rose.

Rose donned her cover once more.

"Two…Hand salute…Two…Left face…Post!"

After going through the commanded motions, Rose marched out of the room.

Whit glanced at Worst-gen, who appeared to be seething behind his mask. He sat for a moment, keeping his eyes cast downward on the orange folder bearing the name of Seaman Rose Hartman.

"Let's just pretend for a moment," Worst-gen began in a soft voice that Whit was pretty sure made everyone uneasy, "that there's a proper way in which shit needs to be done in order that we don't all look like fucking assholes."

For a moment, the room was still.

"Petty Officer Duff," Worst-gen continued, without turning his head to face the young supervisor, whom Whit noticed appeared to have a slight tremble in his knees. "Kindly enlighten me as to what your mind's major malfunction was when you asked a fucking accused sailor to make a statement, which was not required of her, and which – in fact – was not taken with the preface that she was not *required* to make such a statement."

"Sir," Duff began in a shaky tone, his massive gut heaving as he tried to muster the words, "we thought she was ready to talk to us about…"

"THAT DOESN'T FUCKING MATTER!" Worst gen exploded. "YOU FUCKERS HAVE PUT ME IN A POSITION NOW WHERE I CAN'T HOLD THIS SAILOR ACCOUNTABLE! I *HAVE* TO DROP THE CHARGES. A STATEMENT NOT MADE VOLUN- TARILY – WITH THE RIGHT PROTOCOLS – IS A STATEMENT THAT CAN INCRIMINATE A SAIL- OR WITHOUT THE PROPER DUE PROCESS HAV- ING BEEN TAKEN! THANKS TO YOU, I'VE NOW GOT A SAILOR WHO WENT OUT DURING CO- VID, MAYBE GOT SICK, POSSIBLY GOT FUCK- KNOWS-WHO SICK AT THIS COMMAND, AND I CAN'T DO A THING ABOUT IT!!!"

Worst-gen then picked up Rose's binder off of the table.

"THIS!" he bellowed. "THIS FUCKING THING RIGHT HERE…IS USELESS NOW, THANKS TO YOU FUCKING GUYS!!!"

With that, he flung the binder to his left, so that it

landed just in front of Duff's feet. On instinct, the hefty sailor jumped back, and almost fell into the chair that was directly behind him.

No one moved; everyone remained at the position of attention.

"And you, JAG!" Worst-gen went on, in a slightly less monstrous voice. "You let this happen."

"I know, sir," she immediately conceded, putting up her hands as if placating a spoiled child. "And I'm sorry."

Whit almost saw tears forming in JAG's eyes.

Worst-gen glared at her, as if trying to maintain the heightened energy level of his tirade and fury. Maybe it was her conciliatory tone, or maybe it was just the fact that it was JAG. Whit guessed the latter, as he watched the Captain steal a cursory glance up and down her lithe figure.

*Sex sells...and it calms the soul.* Whit now thought, as he watched Worst-gen leer angrily at his legal officer.

"You bear responsibility for this too," Worst-gen continued, barely missing a beat, but calming some more as he kept his eyes on JAG. "Don't let it happen again."

"Yes, sir."

A moment, as Worst-gen sat back in his chair, and cast his eyes upward toward the ceiling. He looked at that moment as though he were praying, though Whit of course knew better.

"Bring her back in," the Captain instructed.

The Master-At-Arms opened the conference room door and stood aside of the doorway.

"Accused…enter!"

Moments later, Rose was back in her place.

"Seaman Hartman," Worst-gen began, "due to a technical error in the legal proceedings involving your case, I…" he hesitated, as if having to chew glass shards instead of stating what he had to say next. "…I have no choice but to drop the charges against you."

Worst-gen paused, and Whit glanced at Rose, who seemed to suck in a deep breath into her chest, and emit a sigh of relief.

"Just to be very forthright, though," Worst-gen went on, "the facts of your case are still quite clear. You violated a lawful order, specifically my COVID guidance. You put the lives of countless sailors and families at risk, and in so doing, put yourself on the same moral plane – in my estimation – as a sexual predator. If you think that sounds harsh, I honestly don't give a shit, because it's fucking true.

"Still," he continued, "because – unlike you – *we* at this command observe the rules and regulations around here, again, the choice is out of my hands as to whether or not I can properly hold you accountable. And that's why you're getting off easy…this time."

Rose remained still.

"But mark my words," Worst-gen went on, pointing an index finger and glaring with narrowed eyes, "you're under about the biggest fucking microscope you've ever been under…because of what you've done, Seaman Hartman. You're going to have to prove yourself even harder than you've had to prove yourself already. Because I'm here to tell you: another fuck-up? Another violated order? You so much as get out of your seat in the damn classroom without proper authorization…and I'll boot your ass out of my schoolhouse so fast, you'll probably lose every memory you ever had of that beach house you and your boyfriend went to. Do you understand me?"

"Yes, sir."

"You're on thin ice, Seaman Hartman. And you're out of chances. And I would strongly suggest getting that straight in your mind before you walk out of this conference room."

In true Worst-gen fashion, he rambled on, fussing at Rose for several more minutes. Whit tuned out most of it, and found himself just staring at Andrew Bestgen.

What was it about him? Whit wondered. What was it about men – and women, for that matter – having power that made them abuse it so? Was it the power itself? Or was it something else? Did Worst-gen simply enjoy burning ants under a magnifying glass? Did men like him get their jollies from hurting others who were in no position to fight back? Or maybe it was that they simply saw it as "just part of the job" and were really – despite all the demonstrative evidence to the contrary – dispassionate about all of it. Whit found the latter musing hard to believe as he looked upon the apoplectic, reddened face of his commanding officer.

"You are dismissed." Worst-gen finally said to Rose, as if concluding a business transaction at a local store nearby.

Rose pivoted smartly, and was now facing Whit for the first time. Despite the favorable verdict that she had just received, her appearance was more gaunt and hollow-eyed than Whit had even first suspected. She made eye contact with him, and Whit felt a lump come to his throat. Now it was his turn to fight back tears.

"Post!" ordered the Master-At-Arms, to which Rose responded by marching a few paces toward Whit. When she came to within inches of his face, Whit was afraid – for a moment – that she would collapse right then and there into his arms.

He tried to convey a smile to her from behind the mask he wore. He knew it was to no avail, but at the same time, he felt he had to. It was almost as if he needed to give her something; a gesture of some kind that might, in some small way, assuage the pain and burden to which she had been subjected.

So he smiled, and then gave her a wink.

Rose's tear-stained eyes, ever so slightly, seemed to light up at this. Somehow, Whit had connected with her, and – in an infinitesimal, miniscule way – had let her know that everything was going to be okay; just as he had in his office when they had spoken before.

Rose pivoted in the next moment, and turned to her right as she passed Whit and exited the conference room.

Whit watched her go and said a short prayer.

Whit was the first one out, and made his way to the first floor – the quarterdeck – where his office was located.

The Site chaplain's office was actually two offices in one. The outer office closest to the hallway served as both a work space for Whit's chaplain assistant as well as a waiting area. It was a small area that often had a cramped feel to it; only two chairs – the desk chair for the assistant, and a chair for sailors to sit in as they waited for the chaplain. Yet, it was still cozy, and it provided students a place to sit and decompress as they waited for their appointments.

As Whit entered, Ensign Patrick Nichols – "Nick," as he was often referred to – greeted him from the outer office desk.

"Hey, Chaps," Nick said. "How's your morning?"

"It was a bitch," Whit answered. "Which is to say JAG's a bitch, per usual. And Worst-gen's a prick."

Nick nodded, and was more than willing to overlook Whit's breach of etiquette. Calling a colleague a "bitch" and your commanding officer a "prick" often generated looks involving raised eyebrows and mouths agape, and – worse – could also lead to trouble. But those rules did not apply in Whit's office; certainly not as long as Worst-gen was commander.

Ensign Patrick Nichols knew this better than anyone. He himself had suffered at Worst-gen's hands more than most people currently at the Site. After an off-campus get-together that Nick and a few of his friends had organized, things had been found out, names had been taken, and Nick – along with a few others – had been hauled before the captain to answer for their COVID crimes.

The result had not been pretty.

Nick was in the process of being dismissed from the program, and it was for this reason that he had been relegated to working temporarily as Whit's assistant. Once his transition to another profession within the Navy was complete, he would be out of the Site, and likely out of Charleston – something that he was eagerly awaiting.

As was his nature, Whit felt terrible for him. Like most of the people who had been caught in Worst-gen's (and JAG's) COVID web, Nick was hardly a bad person, regardless of what the commander had said about him during his Mast. And as if to prove the point, Nick had never wasted time feeling sorry for himself. Instead, after being assigned to work as Whit's assistant, Nick had gone right to work and always went above and beyond his regular duties. He did extra chores while manning the desk; he cleaned; he rearranged furniture when it was necessary;

he procured office odds and ends that were needed; any-thing that needed to be done, he did, and without any complaints.

And the best part about the whole business was that he usually did these things without ever being asked.

Whit respected his assistant more than most people at the command.

"You had a phone call while you were up there," Nick told him. He held out the piece of paper in his hand, which Whit accepted.

As Whit read it, his memory was jarred from the numbness generated by Captain's Mast, and he managed a grin.

"Guy named Geraldo Cisneros," Nick clarified, recit-ing from the card. "Says you guys used to serve together."

"No kidding," Whit said, his mind going to another world.

"I take it you remember him," Nick said.

"Sure do," Whit said, going into his office and closing the door.

Suddenly the day seemed brighter, as Whit picked up the receiver on his phone and dialed the number.

# PART THREE

# DAVIDITY

—————— oOo ——————

# CHAPTER 9

The year was 2012 – early 2012.

The place was the southern region of Afghanistan.

Chaplain Whit Gregg, in his first tour as a Navy chaplain, had just finished playing a pick-up game of football with a few of the other officers and enlisted marines near headquarters and berthing.

Sergeant Geraldo Cisneros had been the quarterback for Whit's team, and had connected with Whit for a short touchdown earlier that afternoon.

Afterward, the two had hit it off after speaking at length. In the course of that conversation, "Raldo" had confided to Whit regarding some issues that he was having back home. Whit had a hard time remembering the specifics, but did remember praying with his Marine friend, and being thanked profusely afterward.

The memory passed through his memory like a song as he sat in his office, dialed the number, and waited for Raldo to pick up.

"Hello," came the subdued, male voice with a Hispanic accent.

"Raldo, how's it going?" Whit responded. "It's Chaps."

"*Mi vato!*" Raldo exclaimed. "Thanks for calling me back, Chaps. It's been a while."

"*De nada,*" Whit responded. "It has been a while."

"Still got that redneck accent," Raldo laughed. "Really comes out when you try to speak Spanish."

Whit smiled, and they made small talk for several moments. As they did, Whit remembered that his post-football talks with Raldo had been one of the rare highlights of that deployment. And speaking to him on this morning amidst the frustration he felt with his current unit was beyond refreshing.

After a moment, Whit asked, "So has life been good to you since we got back from the sandbox all those years ago?"

There was silence, maybe a hesitation, before Whit heard him answer.

"Gotta be honest, Chaps," Raldo began, his voice steady, "things ain't so good."

Another pause.

"I'm sorry to hear that," Whit told him.

Silence.

"I'm guessing that's what you called to talk about."

No response.

"Raldo, you there?"

Whit heard no verbal response, but caught the faintest, muffled sound of sniffling, and maybe a faint sob.

"I'm sorry, Chaps," Whit heard Raldo say in a choked voice. "It's really good to hear from you."

"Yeah, same here," Whit tried to reassure him, touched that his presence – even by phone – meant so much to someone. "Take your time, though."

Then Whit was silent. A strategic pause.

Moments later, Raldo spoke again. "I'm sorry," he apologized once more. "But I needed to talk to someone, and frankly Chaps, you're the only person I could think of to turn to. All that time we spent in Afghanistan…" his voice trailed off.

"Yeah," Whit said, remembering.

"I'll be honest with you," Raldo continued, "I'd much rather talk face-to-face, which is kind of impossible given the circumstances."

"Where are you right now?" Whit asked.

"Palm Beach, Florida," Raldo answered.

*Impossible is right*, Whit thought.

Raldo then added, "My boss works me pretty hard, so getting to Charleston would be a challenge, travel restrictions or not."

"What kind of work do you do?"

"Security," Raldo answered. "Private security."

"For who?" Whit asked.

"That's what I need to talk to you about."

The Site had its own recreation center, which sat off of the main building, but was within walking distance. Fifteen minutes after the phone conversation, Whit was sitting inside the gym complex of the rec center and using the Wi-Fi to connect with Raldo on his laptop via the video chat link that he had been sent.

Such was life in 2020. In addition to having to do nearly everything via remote video, Whit also had to be careful about being inside the rec center, the use of which was heavily restricted due to the Captain's mandates. He had doffed his mask – a big no-no anywhere on Site property – because he could scarcely breathe in the damn thing, let alone have a video conversation with someone.

After powering up his computer, and connecting to the internet, Whit opened the email from Raldo containing the link, went through all of the protocols for signing in, and waited. As he did so, he plugged in a set of ear buds to ensure privacy.

Moments later, he was ushered into the private chat room that he and Raldo would use.

"Hey, Chaps," Raldo greeted him.

Whit returned the greeting and gave a slight wave.

Raldo was in his late thirties now, and – certainly in the face - was showing all of the signs of middle age. His hair was thinning, and was now peppered with hints of gray, along with a few wrinkles in the forehead. Whit's own facial rendering, showing in the display window of the video chat, was not much different. What was different, he noticed, were the eyes. For all of his own mid-life struggles, Whit saw that his own eyes were not possessed of the same gaunt look of deep sadness that he saw reflected in Raldo's.

It troubled him.

"You look great," Whit told him, but only because he felt he had to.

"You're breaking the Ten Commandments, Chaps," Raldo said, managing a wry smile. "Chaplains shouldn't lie."

Whit gave a faint smile and said, "Tell me what's going on, Raldo."

Raldo took a deep breath. "I've been spending the last fifteen or so minutes trying to decide *where* to begin exactly."

Whit nodded.

After a long pause, Raldo continued, "Best place would probably be right where you and I left off all those years ago in Afghanistan. You remember those silly-ass football games we played, right?"

Whit smiled and nodded. "How could I forget the Cisneros-to-Gregg connection for six?"

Raldo smiled for the first time. "That's right. We'd play a while and then chat afterwards; one of the highlights of that deployment, as far as I'm concerned."

Whit managed a smile as he remembered, and wondered to himself why hard memories were often so successful at marginalizing pleasant ones. Why was that the case, and why was it not the case that he could immediately remember the football games and life-changing chats with Raldo, which he was recollecting now?

"Do you remember what we talked about during those times?" Raldo asked him.

Whit struggled with his memory once more. "Vaguely," he answered. "I remember that it was family-related."

Raldo nodded. "Back then, I was having a hard time with my wife – she's my ex-wife now - and my little girl."

"I remember now," Whit affirmed. "And I'm sorry."

"Reyna was six," Raldo went on, his eyes trailing off as he walked through the memory. "Her mother and I were headed for divorce then, and we finally ended things after I got back. For a while, we had a joint-custody agreement, but that ended up not working out. Truth was, it began to stop working out right before we deployed."

"I remember," Whit nodded. *Reyna. "Queen" in Spanish, as Raldo had said.*

"A lot of why it stopped working out was because of me. My drinking, to be specific. My ex-wife never could handle it – hell, who could? That's what fucked up our marriage…excuse my language."

Whit nodded.

"And it's what led her, in the end, trying and get me

out of the picture, which she was able to do." Raldo said this almost as if he were trying to get it out with as little pain as possible. "Joint agreement was terminated ultimately, on the grounds of my being an unfit parent. She got full custody, and I stopped being able to see Reyna."

Whit frowned, and managed to fight back tears of his own as he watched Raldo's eyes well up through the screen.

"I didn't see her for years after we got back."

"I'm sorry."

A moment of silence passed before either of them said anything.

"Let me ask you something, Chaps," Raldo finally said, his eyes filled with a pleading sadness. "Have you ever regretted something so deeply that you wanted to give your life to reverse it?"

Whit thought about his own life for a moment. He thought about the years he had spent in the Navy, and how much heartache and angst he had experienced as a result. However, something told him that his own experience paled in comparison to what Raldo was sharing with him now.

"I can't honestly say that I ever have," he answered Raldo.

"My drinking," Raldo went on, tears now rolling down his cheeks, "killed my marriage."

Whit just sat and listened, waiting for whatever was next.

"And it's also what killed my daughter."

"What?" Whit almost gasped.

Raldo was sobbing now. "She killed herself…" he bawled through the screen, "after being sexually abused by my boss…Carson Pelagius."

*Maddy and Rae – the new girl with the crown birth-mark - had just gone to the back, accompanied by Giselle.*

*Raldo stood looking at the door.*

*One glance, one glimpse of that crown-shaped birthmark, and he was certain he knew.*

*It was Reyna…it had to be Reyna. It was why he had recognized the scent of the perfume – Reyna's mother's – which Saundra had worn during their honeymoon.*

*Something impelled him. Forced him. He had to verify it…if only just one more time.*

*Without a second thought, Raldo strode forward and knocked on the door leading to the back room where they had gone.*

*He waited, and was about to knock a second time when Giselle answered. As the door opened, she gave him a look that demanded a reason for why he was standing there…intruding.*

*"What is it, Raldo?" she pressed.*

*Raldo took a deep breath. "That girl," he almost stammered. "The new one."*

*Her eyes bore into him, demanding clarification. "What about her?"*

*"Do you know her real name?"*

*Giselle's spine stiffened, and Raldo braced for a scolding.*

*"She looks familiar is all," he managed to get out quickly. It was the best he could do.*

*"This is irregular, Raldo," Giselle scolded him.*

*Raldo's mind fought through the shock and fog, and he struggled to fabricate an excuse. "Security," he said. "If she is familiar, to me or to anyone, I'm the security head, and I should probably know about it, so that I can advise the boss before he does anything with her."*

*Giselle's eyes narrowed, and her dark complexion seemed even more ominous than usual in the soft light of the house's interior. An uncomfortable moment passed before she said anything more.*

*"Maddy would know. Let me ask," she said abruptly, and shut the door in his face.*

*Raldo stood there, his hands trembling…waiting.*

*Moments passed like weeks as he stood there, wondering if he'd perhaps seen a mirage when he had seen that birthmark.*

*He wanted it to be a mirage.*

*All he could do was wait.*

*The doors opened again and Giselle reappeared.*

*"Reyna Cisneros," she said.*

*The name landed on his ears like a grenade explosion, and Raldo fought to steady his balance.*

*"That name ring any bells with you?" she asked.*

*It would not even register with Raldo until much later that Giselle had somehow missed the possibility that there might be a family connection. She knew Raldo's full name, and now knew the girl's name. Somehow it had escaped her.*

*Raldo could barely stand on his own two feet. As he struggled to steady himself, he looked past Giselle and into the room where the girls had gone with Giselle to visit Pelagius.*

*Reyna was there, in sight. She was barely visible from behind a wall that led to the inner sanctum, where she would meet Pelagius, and give him whatever sick thing he desired from her that evening. But at that moment, he could see her, and she could see him.*

*She stood there, gazing back at him with large, frightened eyes; ones that recognized; ones that somehow knew.*

*Raldo kept his gaze fixed on his daughter through that doorway; and his eyes met hers.*

*What happened next he knew he would remember for the rest of his wasted life.*

*Reyna's tiny, delicate lips pursed into a terrified frown, and she – ever so faintly – mouthed a solitary word that Raldo read perfectly.*

*"Papi."*

*Giselle had closed the door, and Raldo could hear her ushering Reyna, his daughter, to the back for her rendezvous with Carson Pelagius.*

*All he could do was stand here, his profound shock giving way only to what felt like a certain nihilistic dread and hopelessness. He stood, staring at the door, feeling like a complete fool. Yes. He was a fool whose own daughter had now fallen into the same trap that he had been a part of; hell, that he had helped set.*

*No matter how small a role he played, Raldo knew that in some terrible, twisted way, he – and perhaps he alone, was responsible for this.*

*He was responsible, and now he was paying.*

*God, how had this happened?*

*How had fate allowed this to happen?*

*Raldo just stood there before the closed door that had been slammed in his face by someone with more power over him.*

*And that was it. At that moment, Geraldo Cisneros no longer felt the shock and bewilderment that he had experienced only moments earlier, at the mention of his lost daugh-*

*ter's name. Those emotions had been eclipsed by something far more dreadful.*

*A feeling of powerlessness.*

*Raldo stood there, at that moment, feeling powerless to save his daughter.*

*An hour later, the doors remained closed, with Reyna still on the other side of them, having God only knew what done to her.*

*She was trapped…he was trapped…and there was nothing either of them could do about it.*

*That word she mouthed kept coming back to him.*

*Papi.*

*Over and over again it played, like a broken movie reel; each replay like a dagger in whatever remnant of a fatherly heart Raldo knew he possessed.*

*His own father had been a drunk, so had he. And so Raldo's mind went to the Generational Curse. Was it truly a real thing? It felt real at that moment. He had grown up with a mocking disdain for such foolishness. Generational Curses, handing down sins from the father to his children, all of that nonsense had seemed inconsequential to him.*

*And yet now, as he sat in this beachside mansion, a house that had somehow become a prison in the last hour, he wondered if he should have taken the folklore seriously.*

*His own daughter. Reyna. "Mi reyna pequena," as he and Saundra had both unofficially christened her on the day of her birth; the cherubic baby girl, destined to be royalty (their royalty), who even had a crown-shaped birthmark.*

*Pelagius had her; was having her, thanks to the Generational Curse.*

*His nightmare was broken by the sound of the double doors being flung open with a bang, as Giselle appeared again.*

*"Raldo, we need you!" she announced in a terrified tone.*

*"What?" he said, without even thinking.*

*"It's the new girl," Giselle responded in a frantic tone. "She's slit her throat."*

# Chapter 11

"My little girl killed herself," Raldo sobbed to Whit through the screen, "right there in that God-forsaken house."

Whit's frantic wiping of his own tears was no match for how fast they were coming. "I'm so sorry," he told Raldo. He had listened for the past hour as Raldo had told him the entire story; rehab, meeting Giselle, the beachfront mansion, Pelagius and his crimes against the girls, Reyna, all of it.

A moment passed, as both men fought to gather the composure to continue.

"I could have stopped her," Raldo continued, using his sleeve against his eyes. "I should have stopped her."

"Why didn't you?" Whit asked after a moment. "Not that I'm judging you, Raldo, but why didn't you?"

Raldo thought for a moment. "I honestly don't know. Shock, maybe. But I can't say for sure."

Whit nodded.

"When I saw her," Raldo went on, "when I saw her mouth the word, *Papi*, it's like it froze me right there where I was standing. Like I could barely move."

Whit took this in as he fought to process all that he had heard. He checked his watch; his next counseling appointment inside the Site building was not for another hour.

On the screen, Raldo seemed to be collecting himself and preparing to speak again.

"When Giselle came running into that room, and told me what had happened…"

"Go on," Whit urged.

"I blacked out," Raldo continued. "Just fainted, man."

Neither of them said anything for a moment.

"When I came to," Raldo went on, "Giselle and Carson were standing over me, and I'll never forget what Pelagius looked like at that moment."

Raldo said this with almost a chuckle; the closest to light-heartedness that Whit had seen him since the conversation had started.

"He was whiter than a ghost. Standing there in his bathrobe, looking as though he was about to die himself. And there I am, laying on the ground, trying to figure out how much of what I had just heard was a dream, and how much of it was real."

He paused.

"They told me what happened; said she'd killed herself

right after Pelagius had finished with her. Said she didn't even hesitate; she was so traumatized by all of it that she just…my little girl."

He paused and shook his head, stifling fresh sobs and wiping away tears.

"That was when they put me on leave," Raldo said. "Giselle and Pelagius told me to go home. Had a doctor check me over, and then sent me out of there. That's where I've been ever since."

"And your daughter?" Whit asked.

"They got rid of her body," Raldo said, his expression somewhere between stoic and indignant. "They called a guy; one of their operatives who solves problems for them when they come up."

Whit's eyes were wide with terror.

"You've got to understand, Chaps," Raldo said, "these characters can make people disappear. It's what money and power does for you…does to you."

Raldo nodded, and Whit saw that fresh tears were forming in his eyes as his breath began to increase. He was losing it again.

"My baby girl," he began to sob. "They didn't do anything for her except get rid of the criminal evidence she might have created for them. All I did was faint like a little bitch, and freeze up, while they took her to some fucking landfill."

Whit wanted to burst in with some heated advice on

achieving justice…*go to the police!…get the FBI involved!…do something!*…but he controlled himself…and he waited.

Whit Gregg sat there and watched his friend fall apart in front of him on his computer screen, and a new reality began to dawn on him: this was by far the most challenging and soul-testing counseling session of his entire career; and would probably likely remain so for some time…if not forever.

And so he waited; knowing that waiting was the challenge. Could he really "sit with the broken" and be a "ministry of presence," as he had heard it put so many times? Could he shut up long enough to do so? Could he refrain from giving advice when it was not needed? At that moment, all he needed to do – regardless of what he *wanted* to do – was sit there with Geraldo Cisneros…if only from a distance.

"I don't know what to do," Raldo said. "Cops don't arrest folks like Pelagius, and besides, he's got people on his payroll to clean up stuff like this; ex-cops who know how to remove evidence."

Whit just sat, nodded, affirmed, and wept.

Moments passed.

"Whit, you said it yourself," Raldo finally said. "You've got daughters, just the same as me. So I need you to do me a favor."

"What's that?"

Through the screen, Raldo looked him dead in the eyes, and said, "I want you to turn off whatever side of your brain or heart makes you think like a chaplain, or a Navy officer, or whatever the hell you usually try to think of yourself as."

Whit nodded.

"And just, for a moment, think like a dad."

"Okay."

"Seriously, man, you're the one person I trust in all of this. The way you took care of me and the guys when we were in Afghanistan; I'll always be indebted to you, and I'll always value your opinion and advice. And that's why I'm asking you now: if you were in my situation right now, what would you do, as a father?"

Whit stared back at Raldo, and saw nothing but his pleading eyes.

"What would you do?" Raldo repeated

Whit thought about his answer. He thought about his Bible, about his career as a minister and chaplain.

And then he stopped.

Those thoughts were soon eclipsed by faces. Female faces. Whit saw the faces of Ava, and Esther, and Rachel, and Rose Hartman, and little Courtney from kindergarten, and the girl with the glue on the bus. He even thought of his own mother. Faces of the women he had known in his life floated to the surface of his mind, and he considered them all…before he finally answered.

"Davidity," he said, without even realizing what he was saying.

"What did you say, Chaps?" Raldo asked.

"Davidity," Whit repeated. "I'm going to tell you all about it."

"DADDY'S HOME! DADDY'S HOME!" exclaimed Ava and Esther, as Whit walked through the door later that evening.

Being drained after work was nothing new, and he still managed to scoop his girls up, one into each arm, as he came through the door.

"Daddy, can we 'wough-house'?'" asked four-year old Esther, whose "r" sounds still came out sounding like "w's".

"No," Whit said, with a frown on his face. "No rough-house."

Esther's angelic little face almost crumpled into a frown. Then her eyes sparkled, as she saw the twinkle in her daddy's eye. "You're just teasing," she said.

"Can't fool you!" Whit exclaimed, putting both girls on the ground and bolting for the master bedroom.

The girls squealed as they bounded behind him and within seconds, they were romping on top the new king-size bedspread that Rachel had just purchased for their mattress.

"Careful, please!" she admonished from the kitchen, as Whit wrestled with both of the girls on their bed.

After the conversation with Raldo, Whit was almost certain that he would not feel like anything resembling wanting to play or wrestle with the girls. All he would want to do, he was sure, would be to go home, eat just a little food (his appetite had all but vanished) and then hit the rack for the night. "Drained and deeply pained" was the only way he knew how to characterize how he felt after talking to Raldo Cisneros.

And yet Raldo's anguished face remained fixed in his psyche.

Life was fleeting. And God, how could he ever be so arrogant as to ever try to guarantee himself that such a soul-crushing fate as Raldo's could never come to him and his?

So hell yes, he would wrestle with his girls tonight; his lack of energy be damned.

He had fresh bruises by the time it was over, mostly courtesy of Esther, who was pretty strong for a four-year old, and a good wrestler, too. Rachel sent out for Chick-Fil-A, and – even though it was a school night – they later sat on the sofa watching one of the dozens of "Barbie" movies that the girls enjoyed.

Neither of the girls made it through the movie.

Soon both had fallen asleep between their parents, leaving Whit and Rachel to watch as Barbie and friends vanquished the villain on the screen.

*Barbie has Davidity*; the thought came to Whit from seemingly out of nowhere.

"What are you thinking about?" Rachel asked him, as she stroked Ava's hair.

Whit sighed. Most of the evening had been illuminated by laughter, good food, and – he was sure – plenty of positive memories that would live on long past the events of the day. Thus, he didn't want to answer her; wanted instead to keep all the negativity compartmentalized and away from their family and home.

And yet, how could he keep it from her? She was his wife. Plus, part of him *wanted* to tell her. Somehow, it was all like a garbage disposal – gauche as that sounded. Somehow, all of what Raldo had poured into him during their video chat needed to come out. And if she was volunteering, then who was he to turn down her offer?

"I spoke to an old Marine friend, today," he began.

"From Pendleton?"

Whit nodded.

"Anybody I would know?"

"Did I ever tell you about Raldo?"

"The guy you played football with on base when you were deployed?"

"Yep."

"And?"

And…so he told her everything. He had to. Confidentiality be damned. When he had finished, her eyes were brimming with tears, and Whit almost hated himself for even going into it.

"God, that's awful," she stated, cradling Ava closer to her.

Whit was fighting back tears himself. The "Barbie" end credits were rolling, but both of them sat there motionless.

"He asked me," Whit finally said, "what I would do… not as a chaplain, not as an officer. But as a dad."

Rachel kept her red-rimmed eyes on him.

"And I told him," Whit continued, wiping the tears from his own eyes, "that if it cost me my soul's very salvation before God, I would find a way back into that house and kill that motherfucker in cold blood before he could rape another girl."

"Whit…"

"Don't," he warned.

"You actually counseled someone to…"

"Yes."

Rachel started to censure him again, but hesitated.

"I know what you're going to say," he told her. "That it's against the rules, against this, or that, or whatever."

She waited a moment for him to continue. "But…?"

"But I'm tired of following the rules, Rachel. Tired of the COVID rules, tired of watching corrupt people run this country, run our lives, and destroy the very souls of our children…and us."

Whit looked at his wife; her expression was pleading

and sorrowful, and he knew why. She hated his rebellious streak; wanted him to always follow the rules; and knew – almost better than him – the consequences for breaking any of them. There was always a proverbial line, and she toed it better than he ever would.

Still, her imploring look soon gave way to almost a resigned understanding, as she glanced away from him down at Ava, and continued to stroke her hair. Soon, she moved with a ginger motion over to Esther's head, and began fluffing her curly, brown tresses.

"Can you get in trouble for advising him to do that?" she asked. "Especially if he goes through with it?"

Whit thought about it for a moment as he stared straight ahead, not seeing the television, or anything near it.

"I don't know," he answered. "But I hope not."

# CHAPTER 12
# PALM BEACH, FLORIDA – ONE WEEK LATER

He had an extra week of leave still to go, per Giselle's orders, but showing up at the house would not be completely unexpected.

As for his ruse, Raldo knew that it was pretty air-tight, too.

On top of both of those facts, as far as he knew, neither Pelagius nor Giselle even suspected that there was a connection between him and Reyna. For all they still knew, Reyna was just another disposable underage girl of Pelagius's, and Raldo had keeled over due to "dehydration and overwork", according to the doctor who had checked him out before he went on leave.

Raldo was also an insider; gainfully and duly employed by Carson Pelagius, and as such, he had every right to be headed into the house at that moment.

And so he took out his key and unlocked the metal latch, before also putting his hand on the identity scanner. He waited for about two seconds as his prints married up with the sensors before there was a hollow *boop* which unlocked the electromagnetic lock at the top of the doorframe.

Raldo opened and entered.

Over the past week since he had conversed with his former chaplain, Raldo had spent time picking his moment and planning. In addition to a perfect cover for entering the house, he also had the advantage of being intimately familiar with Pelagius's schedule.

He checked his watch; almost 7:00 pm. Just about time for Pelagius to settle in and watch whatever Netflix fascination had his attention at that time. Sometimes Giselle joined him in the spacious sitting area, just off of the "massage parlor", where Raldo's precious daughter had spent the last fateful moments of her life.

And that was exactly where a potential complication might lie. If Giselle was with him, he would have to kill her first…and quickly. But if he was successful, then the odds were good that Pelagius would be shocked into stillness – the way Raldo had been when Reyna had entered the house and he realized it was her.

Raldo almost laughed at the irony (and justice) that such a moment would provide.

As he entered the spacious foyer, which led to a common receiving area, and kitchen, he heard the television in the next room. He paused and listened. Sure enough, he soon heard the laughter of two voices; one male and one female.

*Shit.*

This had to work. He would have to kill them both, and it was not even the perfect crime he was after. Raldo reached into his pocket, felt the folded-up paper, and remembered the note he had penned just before leaving his house about a half hour earlier.

Then he thought of Reyna. *Justice, baby girl. Justice. I'll be with you soon.*

He reached into his other pocket, and felt the silver pendant that he had just bought.

*St. Mary Magdalene…Patron Saint of Women.*

Raldo carried no weapons.

*Courage, Justice…Davidity.* He kept uttering these words almost silently.

*Davidity*…what a word. The word his old chaplain had given him just before they had signed off from their conversation over the video chat a week earlier.

*Davidity. Standing up for those who can't stand for themselves.*

Whit had learned it – he said – from a counselor friend that he had been to see. And now Raldo had taken it on almost as an inward battle cry of sorts.

He tried to breathe and steady himself, but the room

was starting to spin; just as it had when he had fainted on that God-awful day.

But he kept moving, and knew that he could not stop. Soon, he was standing in front of the doorway leading into the sitting area. Through the crack separating the double doors, he could make out the ambient light of the wall-mounted large screen, and could barely hear the muffled voices of Pelagius and Giselle.

In truth, the voices were drowned out partially by the sound of the waves breaking against the shoreline just yards from Pelagius's back patio, which overlooked the beach. The door to the back patio was open, and dusk was setting in as the Atlantic horizon darkened.

Raldo almost prayed that no one was close enough to hear what was about to happen, but then it did not really matter, did it? He knew what he had to do, and he also knew that he was not going out the door in handcuffs.

He knocked lightly, and pushed the door open. Sure enough, Pelagius was sitting at one end of a large, leather sofa, facing the screen, and Giselle sat on the other side. Pelagius smiled as he gave a sideways-backward glance.

"Raldo, what's up, man?" he said. "Thought you'd be home resting."

"Came to get a few things," Raldo said, fighting against his racing heart rate.

"Yeah?"

"What things?" Giselle asked, curious, as she munched

on handfuls of popcorn from a bowl in her lap. She did not look his way, and was transfixed on the new western show that their eyes were glued to.

"Think I left my wallet here," Raldo lied, coming into the room, and standing behind the sofa, where they sat.

"Mmm," she said, keeping her eyes glued to the screen.

"How are you feeling?" Pelagius asked, nodding backwards in Raldo's direction, but not putting his eyes on him.

"I'm all right," Raldo said.

"Took quite a fall last week," Pelagius said. "We were worried about you."

*As if you could ever be worried about anybody besides yourself, you fucking sociopath.*

"Yeah."

"You'll be glad to hear," Pelagius said, turning around to face him for the first time, "that we cleaned everything up with that girl last week. Got some guys to dispose of the body. So she's not our problem anymore."

"Yeah," Raldo said, with a calmness that surprised even himself.

Raldo saw blood. Red blood. It covered, in that moment, everything in his world; everything in his line of sight.

*Mary Magdalene, pray for me…give me Davidity.*

His sight narrowed, his focus became tunneled, and his eyes came to light upon Giselle's slender neck, which protruded – along with her head – from just above the top of the sofa. She sat perfectly still, eating popcorn and watching the television. But Raldo only saw her neck.

*For Rayna.*

Then he pounced.

With nary a sound, he lurched forward, grabbed Giselle by the chin and back of the head, and – before she could react – snapped her neck. The bowl of popcorn spilled as he jostled her, which caused Pelagius to divert his eyes from the screen and look over.

Just as Raldo had predicted, Pelagius froze as he saw the unlikely sight of his female confidant's suddenly lifeless body slumped sideways over the arm of the sofa.

"What?...Raldo?" he said, his brain seemingly disengaged from his mouth.

In shock, he looked up at Raldo, who had not hesitated, and was now grabbing Pelagius by the gray sweatshirt that he wore and catapulting him over the back of the sofa with a mighty pull.

Within seconds, Carson Pelagius was fully subdued under the bulk of Geraldo Cisneros. The larger man deadlocked one of his knees into Pelagius's throat, and pinned his arms back with both of his hands.

For the briefest of moments, Pelagius fought to mount a resistance, but Raldo's strength was too much. He squirmed like a dying rabbit in the jaws of a coyote.

The lights were out in the sitting room, and it was

almost pitch dark outside, but Raldo looked with satisfaction upon his new victim, and noted the shock and tears that were starting to form in his eyes. Whether they were for Giselle, or out of sheer, cowardly, punk-ass fear, who was to say? It did not matter. Raldo knew that he himself would die – in just a few moments – a happy man, knowing that he had reduced this pitiful little evil man who had killed his daughter to a hapless, blubbery waste right before he killed him.

"Guess what, Pelagius?" Raldo almost whispered. "That 'problem' you think you solved? You ain't solved it like you thought you did, you little bitch."

Pelagius gaped at him bewilderedly, struggling to make sense of it; hell, at that moment, he was struggling to breathe as Raldo kept the knee buttressed against his trachea.

"Wanna know why? I'll tell you why. Because that girl that died, here in your house, while you were RAPING HER?" he jammed his knee deeper into Pelagius's throat as he said those last two words. "That girl, the one you say was a problem you solved…"

He paused for a moment, giving Pelagius time to make sense of what he was saying to him.

"That girl," he said, "was my daughter."

Pelagius's eyes looked as though they would bulge out of his head as Raldo uttered this last sentence.

"That's right, you sick fuck," he said to him. "Reyna Evangelina Martita Cisneros! That was her name. And it's the last thing you're going to hear before I take your miserable, fucking life."

Pelagius emitted what sounded like a grunt of protest, as his eyes grew even wider, it seemed, and tears began to well up within his lower eyelids. He was gasping and sobbing all at once, as Raldo kept his menacing gaze upon him.

"Reyna…Evangelina…Martita…Cisneros!"

With that, Raldo let go of one of Pelagius's hands and, in an instant, drew back a fist and brought it back down upon his victim's face, right between his terrified eyes. There was a dual *crack-cracking* sound as the blow landed, and Pelagius's head smacked against the tile floor.

Pelagius was both injured and stunned by the blows, and could mount no resistance, even though Raldo had freed one of his hands.

Raldo raised his fist again, and slammed it down into Pelagius's face once more in another sickening *thwack*. Following this, Raldo continued his assault with a barrage of blows.

"Reyna…"

*Thwack.*

"Evangelina…"

*Thwack.*

"Martita…"

*Thwack.*

"Cisneros…"

*Thwack.*

"Reyna…"

*Thwack.*

"Evangelina…"

*Thwack.*

"Martita…"

*Thwack.*

"Cisneros…"

*Thwack.*

He kept the devastating punches coming, one right after the other, and in succession with each time he used one of his dead daughter's appellations. On and on he went, destroying the man who had killed his daughter, the bones in his own hand breaking – shattering – even as he was crushing Pelagius's facial structure, and drawing gobs of red blood from his nose, mouth, eyes, and other open wounds.

He kept going until he was certain he could go no more.

When he stopped, he just sat there for a moment, his knee still on the neck of the pulverized Carson Pelagius, whose erstwhile handsome face had gone from battered and swollen, to bloody, to pulpy, to all four…

…and finally lifeless.

Raldo checked for a pulse just to make sure.

*Dead as roadkill,* he mused inwardly, to his own satisfaction.

Then he looked around. He knew the odds were good that he would be the only one in the house besides Giselle and Pelagius, but he also knew that it was impossible to be one-hundred percent sure.

And so Raldo rose, keeping his eye on the mess he had just created. Pelagius lay in a lifeless heap just beneath where he now stood, and Raldo marveled at how clean he looked from the neck down. His gray sweatshirt, and matching sweatpants – *such a damned '80s look* – had not the first drop of blood or grime on them. But his face looked like something out of a Hollywood horror studio, and his head was encircled with a halo of gore.

Raldo stood in front of him, nodded, and then whispered, *That's for you, baby…for you, mi Reyna pequena.*

Then he cried.

Why? He was not sure. Maybe it was the onset of the realization that Reyna was still dead, and that he would never reconcile with her, and nothing could change that. He would never walk her down the aisle, never attend graduations, or birthdays, or holidays, or – perhaps worst of all – the birth of his own grandchildren.

All of that was still gone; and would remain gone. All of it had been robbed from him by the two monsters whom he had just slain.

It was an empty sensation, and one he would not wish on anybody.

It was time to die.

Raldo went to a cabinet near the entrance to the massage parlor, opened it, and reached up onto the top shelf. He felt the cold steel and smiled to himself.

Retrieving the Colt .45 that he had known for some time was there, he took it onto the back porch and sat in a deck chair. Remembering the moments over the past four years brought him a modicum of peace. As he reflected on the times he had dreamed of Reyna, of being with her again, of watching the remainder of her growing up, of all that hope he had once had to himself, he felt the emptiness dissipate – only for a moment – and he actually felt himself smile.

Raldo put the gun on the ground and reached into his pockets once more. He felt both the note he had written earlier, and the St. Mary Magdalene pendant that he had bought for cheap earlier that day. Everything was in place, and was just where it needed to be once his body was discovered.

He was smiling as he picked the gun back up, and checked the magazine port to make sure it was loaded. And he continued smiling as he chambered a round, and opened his mouth to insert the muzzle of the pistol.

The memory of a dark-haired girl running toward him and leaping into his arms came to his mind and remained there.

*Te quiero mucho, Papi. Eres mi heroe!*

Reyna's angelic voice was the last thing that Geraldo

Cisneros thought of in the split-second that he pulled the trigger, firing the bullet into his brain, and ending his life.

# Chapter 13

The inspector's name was Regis. He examined the body, and carefully looked over the note that had been found only moments earlier.

A late-night beachcomber had called the police when they heard gunfire coming from the Pelagius estate.

As the authorities entered, some of them were taken aback at the grisly scene.

Regis, however, was a veteran and remained stoic as he examined the paper, taking every precaution to keep his gloved hands from contaminating anything.

The note read:

*"To Whom It May Concern:*

*It may seem like the coward's way, but I assure you it is not. These animals — one Carson Pelagius and one Giselle Masterson — raped dozens of young girls, including my daughter, Reyna Evangelina Martita Cisneros, who killed herself as a result. I have no idea where her body is, but if you're worth your salary, maybe you can find out. And please try to do so;*

*she deserves a proper burial, so that her mother can grieve the way she's supposed to. It's the least I can give her after all this time, and all that I've put her through. The least you all can do for me — especially since you routinely refuse to prosecute sex-trafficking pricks like these — is find her.*

*I want to say to my family that I love you all, and I'm sorry. This isn't how I wanted to go out; but it had to be done… for Reyna. I hope to see you all on the other side some day.*

*To Chaplain Whit Gregg, mi vato, thank you, brother. We'll always have Afghanistan, touchdowns, the counsel that you've so graciously provided me…and the Davidity; the ability to stick up for others who can't stick up for themselves. Thank you for showing me what that's about. You're a good man. God bless you.*

Always,
Geraldo Enrique Cisneros,
USMC (Semper Fi)

"Yes, sir," Whit told the investigator over the phone later that week. He closed his eyes, and tried to ignore the filth that he felt at what he was about to say. "I would start by checking the landfills around the Palm Beach area."

*Landfills…these monsters.*

"Yes, sir," he continued. "I hope you find something

out, soon. From what I've been hearing, Pelagius was the tip of the iceberg; he had a lot of folks come to him with the desire to abuse these girls, too. I hope you bring them all down."

Moments later, they hung up, and Whit rubbed his eyes, praying that the information he had given would lead to a breakthrough of some kind.

*...she deserves a proper burial, so that her mother can grieve the way she's supposed to. It's the least I can give her after all this time.* That part of Raldo's suicide note was the part that Whit knew he would always remember.

It was the least he could do for Raldo.

The hallway just outside of his office was buzzing with activity; Site students coming and going, all of them oblivious to the hell that Whit himself was experiencing and going through at that moment.

But Whit heard none of it. His mind was on Raldo.

Raldo's death.

Raldo's suicide note.

Whit got up and went outside the building so that he could cry in peace. All of the news was overwhelming, but at that moment, Whit could only grieve for his friend.

He sat in his office later, and rubbed his eyes. Maybe Rachel had been right. Maybe advising Raldo to do what he did had been the wrong thing. Maybe it would come back to haunt him in some fashion; be it sooner or later on.

He kept his head down and only looked up when he heard Nick talking to someone in his outer office.

Whit craned his neck to the side so that he could see out the door, and his heart almost sank.

JAG was standing there; that same, familiar smirk – concealed by a mask – was almost for certain on that pretty, damned face of hers.

With everything going on, and with the inner turmoil he was feeling, he did not know if an encounter – however innocuous – with Jade Kulkarni was something he was able to tolerate at the time.

JAG sashayed into the office, her khakis hugging her curves, and Whit marveled at how someone so attractive could make him so pissed off. He would never love anyone besides Rachel, but damn…he flat out despised Jade Kulkarni more than ever at that moment.

"Hey, Chaps," she practically chirped.

"JAG," Whit rose from his chair. Old habits die hard, especially southern ones. *Always stand when a lady enters.*

She closed the door, and turned to face him again.

"Chaps, I just thought you should know that the command has been notified about your name being mentioned in that Marine's suicide note…the one who killed the rich guy."

Whit nodded.

"We may need you to come in and talk to myself and possibly the regional JAG…maybe higher."

"What for?"

"Procedural stuff," she said. "You're not in trouble…at least not yet…and you shouldn't be in trouble in the long run, either. But it's just a formality."

Whit narrowed his eyes at her. "What do you mean, 'at least not yet'?"

JAG's eyes narrowed, and she kept her gaze on him. "There are whispers," she said. "Rumors at this point, but some folks that I've talked to linked with the investigation, seem to think you might have advised Cisneros to kill Pelagius."

Whit said nothing, but kept his eyes forward.

*Davidity…stay strong.*

"You don't have to make any statement, or say anything incriminating."

"That's because I didn't do anything incriminating," Whit shot back.

"You don't have to get defensive," she retorted. "We're all on the same team here."

A chuckle, one that Whit could not hold back, escaped from his nose and mouth. Then he felt the overwhelming rage from months of suppressed anger rise to the surface.

A sardonic smile crept up onto his face, as he held JAG with a contemptuous glare.

"Same team," he mocked. "Jade, I think it's time you and I got something straight: we're not on the same team. And we never will be, as long as you intimidate and belittle people half the time you're in this building, and spend the other half sucking up to the Captain, and sucking God knows what else in the process."

A look of shock registered on JAG's face.

Then, her shock gave way to anger as her eyes narrowed once more. "That's fine, Chaps. We'll see how the XO feels about what you just said to me."

She stormed out.

Nick appeared in the doorway, his mouth agape, laughter bubbling up from within him.

"Chaps, that was…" he began, then burst out laughing once more. "Awesome!"

Whit just stood there, smiling to himself.

After a good chewing out by the Executive Officer (XO), Whit decided to end his day prematurely, and stop by the grocery store for Rachel on the way home. She needed sour cream for whatever deliciousness she was making that evening, and Whit had happily obliged.

He decided not to tell her about the run-in at work, or about the apology he had been forced to give JAG, or about the fact that he had almost gotten chewed out a second time when he refused to make the apology sound sincere.

Instead, he would just kiss Rachel and the girls as he walked through the door, and spare them the details.

He was making his way through the parking lot to his car when he heard a familiar voice call out.

"Chaplain?"

Whit turned, and smiled as Seaman Rose Hartman approached him. She wore the same camouflage uniform that Whit wore. However, Whit noticed, her face was different. Somehow it was brighter and more vivacious than he had ever remembered it being.

"How have you been?" he asked her.

"Fine. Just getting through Nuke School."

He nodded and grinned. "I'm sure you're glad to still be getting through Nuke School."

"Very."

"How is everything else? Boyfriend doing okay?"

Rose nodded. "Yeah. Sucks that we can't see each other right now, but…"

Whit understood.

"Listen, Chaps, I just wanted to thank you for all that you did for me."

"It's no problem."

"And I brought you this," she continued, reaching into one of her pockets, and pulling out a small plastic bag, which she presented to him.

"Thank you," Whit told her, as he accepted it.

The bag was twist-tied with a ribbon, and as Whit unwrapped it, he noticed that it contained cookies.

"I baked them myself," Rose told him.

"Wow," Whit said. "Won't help me much with the next PFA, but that's why we work out, right?"

Rose chuckled.

"Plus, I can always just give them to my kids."

She smiled and then added, "There's a note in there for you, too."

Whit glanced into the bag again, and sure enough, a small, folded piece of paper was inside. He unwrapped it and began reading.

*Dear Chaplain Gregg,*

*Thank you for helping me through a difficult time in my life. And thank you for being like a second dad to me since I've been here at the Site.*

*You rock!*

*-Seaman Rose Hartman*

Whit reached out and gave Rose a hug.

"Thank you," he told her.

"Thank *you*, Chaps."

They spoke for a few more minutes before parting ways. As Whit continued making his way to the car, he glanced up. The sun was just starting to peek from behind a dense cloud.

"Thank you, God," he whispered.

Whit parked his car in the lot of the food store that was just blocks from his apartment and went inside. He hated to shop, and had soon located what he was looking for before heading for the nearest open checkout aisle.

He was standing in line when a familiar voice said, "Chaplain?"

Whit turned and beamed when he saw who was behind him.

"Dr. Allenby."

The older man, ever ebullient, held out his fist, and Whit bumped it with his own…the new 2020 greeting.

"How are you, Whit?"

"Fine. And you?"

"Just great," he answered, his eyes shining from behind his glasses. "I've been praying for you."

"Thank you," Whit said. "They've been getting answered in some strange ways lately."

Dr. Allenby nodded. "They usually do. How are things with your commander? Any better than before?"

"Not really," Whit shook his head. "He'll never change; most senior officers like him never do."

"That's the truth," Dr. Allenby agreed. Then, changing the subject, Dr. Allenby stated, "So your prayers are getting answered in some strange ways lately, huh?"

"That's right."

"Would this have to do with a certain former Marine that you've recently counseled?"

Whit studied him, and began to feel alarmed. "What have you heard?"

Dr. Allenby cast a furtive glance around the store and then looked back at Whit. "Seems there's a lot of scuttlebutt going on about a certain Marine that made the news recently."

Whit's heart started pounding. How far and wide was his involvement really known?

"Relax, Whit," Dr. Allenby reassured. "One thing about being in my line of work for as long as I have been in it is that you make contacts. You meet people, you touch lives, and those lives branch out and touch others. A relative of someone I counseled long ago and built a relationship with was part of the investigative team down in Florida. When they saw 'Davidity' mentioned in that note he wrote…well…let's just say that word traveled fast, and it eventually traveled back to me."

Whit was taken aback.

"Don't suppose you had anything to do with that, did you?"

Whit had no answer, and looked away with a sheepish grin.

"You've nothing to be ashamed of, Whit," Dr. Allenby said, ever the clairvoyant, it seemed. "What happened to Sergeant Cisneros was tragic; but you touched his life. Always remember that."

After the day he'd had, Whit now felt like crying. He kept his eyes on the elderly man who had helped him… and in turn, enabled him to help a fellow warrior.

"Thank you, Dr. Allenby," he said to him.

"No," Dr. Allenby replied, gesturing upward with his index finger. "Thank God."

The two men hugged, and then said good-bye.

Moments later, Whit rolled into the parking lot, killed the engine, and got out. He glanced across the property complex and noticed two girls climbing a magnolia tree that was planted near their building. It took him only a brief moment to realize that both girls belonged to him, and he fought the urge to call out to Ava and Esther right away. He knew that they would run headlong toward him, and jump into his arms – which was something he relished, and wanted.

But not right away.

At that moment, he just stopped and watched them; took in their innocence, their carefree and uninhibited nature, as Ava first scaled the lowest-hanging magnolia branch, followed by her not-to-be-outdone younger sister. Esther, in her typical bravado, used both hands and her legs to monkey her way onto the same branch that her sister now sat on.

*Somewhere out there*, his mind suddenly turned dark, *another Pelagius. Another monster. Just waiting to rob them of their innocence.*

He felt his angst rising again; all of the negativity he had felt while listening to Raldo's gripping story about his daughter, about his life; all of the negativity he had experienced with his command, and their inability to affirm the dignity of anyone that ran afoul their ridiculous COVID rules. He felt his anger starting to boil over.

And then, without even realizing it, without even being *conscious of it*, he began to hear his own voice.

"Davidity," he said, just above a whisper. "Defense… of the innocent. My life's purpose."

Like a mist, the anger and negativity dissipated, and he was free again.

"GIRLS!!!" he bellowed.

As if on an automation of some kind, Ava and Esther both looked up in rapt attention at the sound of their daddy's voice, as he stood in the parking lot next to his car. Both of them exchanged glances and then, with the speed and dexterity that only children can muster, they both scrambled down out of the tree and began tearing across the grass, which gave way to the parking lot, in the direction of Chaplain Whit Gregg's open arms.

As they ran, they shrieked out in joyful peals.

"DADDDDDYYYYYY!!!!!!"

Whit beamed as they got closer and closer, and then gathered them both up in a bear hug.

## SOUL SPRINTS

By John W. Gibson

"Lake Barrow, Florida is a small, central Florida farming community which prides itself on loving three things: faith, family, and the mighty Spartans of Sims County High. The tiny Bible-belt town is also home to a long-standing feud between two of its most prominent families, the Gills and the Danforths.

Jayce Leonard is a hometown football hero from Lake Barrow who is all too familiar with the Gill-Danforth controversy. After achieving success as a college quarterback at a small university, Jayce is called home in 2003 to coach at his alma mater at the age of twenty-four, making him the youngest high school head coach in the state of Florida. However, he soon finds himself squarely in the middle of his hometown's checkered history again as he seeks to start a family and successfully lead his beloved Spartans on the gridiron. Alongside him is his college teammate and best friend, Soul Rasheed. "Coach Soul," as he is known to the team, is a Muslim and former favorite receiving target of Jayce's whose enthusiasm and charisma quickly endear him to the players. However, Soul's presence in Lake Barrow - along with his faith - soon generates fresh strife in the midst of the ongoing discord that has plagued Jayce's small town for years.

*Soul Sprints* is a football tale of love, friendship, tolerance, and the ties of family and community that bind, even in the unceasing presence of bitterness and prejudice in post-9/11 America."

# Author Bio

I am the award-winning author of six books, a lifelong resident of northwest Florida, a teacher, minister, and chaplain in the Navy Reserves. I enjoy reading, exercising, and spending time with my family.